ALFRED HITCHCOCK'S

WITCH'S BREW

Here is a heady brew of shivery occult tales by eleven expert storytellers. Witches are the main ingredient, and to add spice, master chef Alfred Hitchcock has also stirred in two fortunetellers, a modernized vampire, and the Devil himself! So if you're not afraid to try a taste of something new, turn the page and proceed to the feast.

Alfred Hitchcock Story Collections
for Young Readers

ALFRED HITCHCOCK'S

WITCH'S BREW

Random House New York

The editor wishes to thank the following for permission to reprint:

"The Wishing Well" by E. F. Benson. Reprinted by permission of the Estate of the late E. F. Benson.

"That Hell-Bound Train" by Robert Bloch. Copyright © 1958 by The Mercury Press, Inc. Reprinted by permission of the author and the author's agents, Scott Meredith Literary Agency, Inc., 845 Third Avenue, New York, NY 10022.

"As Gay As Cheese" by Joan Aiken. From *The Far Forests* by Joan Aiken. Copyright © 1977 by Joan Aiken. Reprinted by permission of Viking Penguin Inc.

Chapter 6 from *The Sword in the Stone* ("Madame Mim") by T. H. White. Copyright 1939 by T. H. White; renewed. Reprinted by permission of G. P. Putnam's Sons and A. Watkins, Inc.

"Blood Money" by M. Timothy O'Keefe and "They'll Never Find You Now" by Doreen Dugdale. Copyright by *The London Mystery Selection*. Reprinted by permission.

"His Coat So Gay" by Sterling Lanier. From the book *The Peculiar Exploits of Brigadier Ffellowes*. Copyright © 1972 by Sterling Lanier. Copyright © 1970 by The Mercury Press, Inc. Transferred to Sterling Lanier in 1971. Reprinted by permission of Curtis Brown, Ltd. Abridged from the original.

"The Widow Flynn's Apple Tree" by Lord Dunsany. From *The Sword of Welleran* by Lord Dunsany. Copyright 1954 by Lord Dunsany; renewed 1982. Reprinted by permission of The Devin-Adair Publishing Co., Old Greenwich, CT 06870.

"In the Cards" by John Collier. Copyright 1951 by John Collier; renewed 1979. "The Proof" by John Moore. Copyright 1953 by John Moore; renewed 1981. Both stories reprinted by permission of Harold Matson Co., Inc.

"Strangers in Town" by Shirley Jackson. Copyright © 1959 by Shirley Jackson. Reprinted by permission of Brandt & Brandt Literary Agents, Inc., from *The Saturday Evening Post*. Copyright © 1959 by The Curtis Publishing Company.

The editor gratefully acknowledges the invaluable assistance of Henri Veit in the preparation of this volume.

Library of Congress Cataloging in Publication Data:

Main entry under title: Alfred Hitchcock's Witch's brew.
SUMMARY: An anthology of eleven short stories about magic, witchcraft, and the supernatural. 1. Short stories. [1. Witchcraft—Fiction. 2. Occult sciences—Fiction. 3. Short stories.] I. Hitchcock, Alfred Joseph, 1899–1980. II. Title: Witch's brew.
PZ5.A35894A1 [Fic] 77-74457 ISBN: 0-394-85911-1 (pbk.)

Manufactured in the United States of America 6 7 8 9 0

Contents

To whet your appetite . . .

You have caught me at my newest hobby—cooking. As you will soon see, I have been preparing nothing so ordinary as a mixture of eye of newt and wing of bat with a lizard's egg thrown in for good measure. My cauldron contains a heady brew of occult tales by eleven master storytellers. I venture to say that you will find all of them spellbinding.

Witches are the main ingredient in this potful of stories. And they come in quite a variety of flavors. You will meet a woman who uses a wishing well to work her evil. You will watch an old crone change a prince of a lad into a frog. And you'll shudder at the ideas that a certain forest-dwelling Madame Mim has about what—or should I say *whom?*—to put into her cookpot.

You can see why witches aren't a popular lot. But not all of them are wicked. One perfectly delightful spellworker I know was dreadfully slandered around town just because a nosy neighbor thought she was too clever a housemaid.

I have also raided the spice shelf to add some exotic flavorings to my witch's brew. You'll find that I've stirred in two fortunetellers—a young woman who reads the future with a well-worn deck of cards, and a barber who can feel a customer's fate when he touches his—or her—head. And then there's a modernized vampire, and even the Devil himself! Delightful chaps, both of them, though terrifying on occasion.

I could go on, but I'm sure you're eager to proceed to the feast. So if you are not too timid to try a taste of something new, something beyond everyday experience, turn the page and commence reading.

Alfred Hitchcock

ALFRED HITCHCOCK'S
WITCH'S BREW

The Wishing Well

E. F. BENSON

The village of St. Gervase lies at the seaward base of that broad triangular valley which lies scooped out among the uplands of the north Cornish moors, and not even among the fells of Cumberland could you find so remote a cluster of human habitations. Four miles of by-road, steep and stony, lie between it and the highway along which in tourist-time the motorbuses pound dustily to Bude and Newquay, and eight more separate it from the railhead. Scarcely once in the summer does an inquisitive traveler think it worthwhile to visit a village which his guidebook dismisses with the very briefest reference to the ancient wishing well that lies near the lich gate of the churchyard there. The world, in fact, takes very little heed of St. Gervase, and St. Gervase hardly more of the outer world. Seldom do you see man or woman waiting at the corner, where the road from the village joins the highway, for the advent of the motorbus, and seldom does it pause there to set down one of its passengers. An occasional trolley laden with sacks of coal and cargo of beer barrels jolts heavily down the lane; for the rest the farms of the valley and the kitchen gardens of the cottagers supply it with the needs of life and its few fishing boats bring in their harvest from the sea. Nor does St. Gervase seek after any fruits of science or culture or religion save such as spring from its soil, which furnishes its wise women with herbs of healing for ailing bodies, and from its tradition of spells and superstition of darker sort to be used in the service of love or of vengeance. These latter are not publicly spoken of save in one house at St. Gervase, but are muttered and whispered in quiet consultations, and thus the knowledge has been handed down from mother to daughter since the days when, three centuries ago, a screeching, handcuffed band of women were driven from here to Bodmin, and, after a parody of a trial, burned at the stake.

It was strange that the vicarage, which might have been expected to be unblackened by the smoke of legendary learning, was the one house where magic and witchcraft were openly and sedulously studied, but such study was purely academical, the Reverend Lionel Eusters being the foremost authority in England as a writer on folklore. His parochial duties were light and his leisure plentiful, for a couple of services on Sunday were, to judge by the congregation, sufficient for the spiritual needs of his parish, and for the rest of the week he was busy in the library of the creeper-covered vicarage that stood hard by the lich gate that led to the churchyard. Here, patient but unremitting, he worked at his great book on witchcraft which had engaged him so many years, occasionally printing some subsection of it as a pamphlet: the origin of the witch's broomstick, for instance, had furnished curious reading. He was a wealthy man with no expensive tastes save that for books on his subject, and the big library he had built on to the vicarage had now few empty shelves. Twenty years ago, when ill health had driven him from the chill clays of Cambridge, he had been appointed to this remote college living, and the warm, soft climate and the strange, primitive traditions that hung about the place suited both his health and his hobby.

Mr. Eusters had long been a widower, and his daughter, Judith, now a woman of forty years old, kept house for him. The time of her more marriageable maidenhood had been spent here in complete isolation from her own class, and though sometimes when she saw the courtships and childbirths of the village the sense of what she had missed made a bitter brew for her, she had long known that St. Gervase had cast some spell upon her, and that had a wooer from without sought her he must indeed be a magnet to her heart if he could draw her from this secluded valley into the world that lay beyond the moors. In the few visits she had paid to relations of her father and mother, she had always pined to be home again, and to wake to the glinting of the sun on the gorse-clad hills, or to the bellowing roar of some westerly gale that threw the sheets of rain against the window: a stormy day at home was worth all the alien sunshine, and the sandy beach of the bay with the waves asleep or toppling in, foam-laced and thunderous, was better than the brilliance of southern seas. Here alone her mind knew that background of content which is brighter than all the pleasures the world offers: here every day the spell of St. Gervase was like some magic shuttle weaving its threads through her.

Since her mother's death Judith's days had been of a uniform monotony. Household cares claimed a short hour of the morning, and then she went to the library where her father worked to transcribe his words if he had a section of his work ready for dictation, or to look up endless references in the volumes that lined the room, if he was preparing the notes which formed the material of his dictation. Some branch of witchcraft was always the subject of it, some magical rite for the fertility of the cattle, some charm for child-bearing, some philter for love, or (what had by degrees got to interest her most), one that caused the man on whom a girl's heart was set, but who had nought for her, to wither in the grip of some nameless sickness and miserably to perish. Month by month as her father pushed his patient way forward through the ancient mists, these satanic spells that blighted grew to be a fascination with Judith.

Just now he was deep in an exploration into wishing wells, and there she sat this morning, pencil in hand for his dictation, as he walked up and down the library, glancing now and then at his memoranda spread out on the table.

"These wishing wells," he said, "are common to the whole of early European beliefs, but nowhere do we find that the power which supposedly presided over them was at the beck and call of any chance persons who invoked their efficacy. Only witches and those who had occult powers could set the spell working, and the origin of that spell was undoubtedly satanic, and not till Christian times were these wells used for any purpose but that of invoking evil. The form of these wells is curiously similar; an arch or shelter of stonework is invariably built over them, and in the sides are cut small niches where, in Christian days, candles were placed or thank-offerings deposited. What they were previously used for is uncertain, but they were beyond doubt connected with the evil spells, and I conjecture that the name of the person devoted to destruction was scratched on a coin, or written on a slip of linen or paper, to await the action of the diabolical power. The most perfectly preserved of these wishing wells known to me is that of St. Gervase in Cornwall; its arched shelter is in excellent condition, and the well, as is usual, very deep. The local belief in its efficacy has survived to this day, though its power is never invoked, as far as I can ascertain, for evil purposes. A woman in pregnancy, for instance, will drink of the well and pray beside it; a girl whose lover has gone to sea will scratch her name on a silver coin and drop it into the water, thus insuring his safe return. The village folk are curiously reticent about such practices, but I can personally vouch for cases of this kind. . . ."

He paused, fingering the short Vandyke beard that grew gayly from his chin.

"My dear, I wonder if that is quite discreet," he said to Judith. "But after all it is highly improbable that any copy of my work published by the university at a guinea will find its way here. I think I will chance it. . . . Dear me, the bell for luncheon already! We will resume our work this evening, if you are at leisure, as I have much ready for dictation."

Judith smiled to herself as she paged the sheets. . . . She knew very much more about her father's parishioners than he, for he, scholar, recluse, and parson, only lived on the fringe of their lives, whereas she, in chatty visits to the women who sat and knitted at their cottage doors, had got into real touch with an inner life to which he was a stranger. She knew, for instance, that old Sally Trenair, whose death less than a week ago had been a source of such relief to her neighbors, was universally held to be a witch, and Sally was always muttering and mumbling round the wishing well. None who crossed her will prospered; their cows went dry or threw stillborn calves, their sheep wilted, the atrocious henbane, fatal to cattle, appeared in their fields: so the prudent wished Sally a polite good day, and sent her honey from their hives and a cut of prime bacon when the pig was killed. But from some vein of secretiveness, Judith did not tell her father of such talk, whispered to her over the knitting needles, which would have inclined him to modify his view about the surviving association of the wishing well with evil invocations. It was idle gossip, perhaps, for if you had challenged her to say whether she believed such tales of old Sally, she would have certainly denied it. . . . And yet something deep down in her would have whispered: "I don't only believe: I *know*."

Today, when luncheon was finished, her father returned to his desk and Judith started to walk a couple of miles up the valley to the farm of John Penarth, whose family from time immemorial had owned those rich acres. For the last eight years he and his wife had lived there alone, for their only son, Steven, had gone out to America at the age of sixteen to seek his fortune. But fortune had not sought him, and now, when his father was growing old and his health declining, Steven was coming home with the intention of settling down here. Judith remembered him well, a big handsome boy with the blue of the sea in his eyes and the sunshine in his hair, and she wondered into what sort of man he would have grown. She had heard that he was already come, but though she was curious to see him, the motive for her visit was really the same as that which so often drew her to the Penarth farm, namely, to have a talk with Steven's mother. There was no one, thought Judith, who was so learned in what was truly worth knowing as Mrs. Penarth. She could not have pointed you India on the big globe that stood in her parlor, or have answered the simplest board-school question about Queen Elizabeth, or have added five to four without counting on her fingers, but she had rarer knowledge in the stead of such trivialities. She had the healing touch for man and beast: she stroked an ailing cow and next day it would be at pasture again; she whispered in the ear of a feverish child, plucking gently at its forehead, and pulled the headache out so that the child slept. And she, alone of all the village, paid no court to Sally Trenair nor sought to propitiate her. One day, as she passed Sally's cottage, Sally had screamed curses on her, and followed her, yelling, halfway to the farm. Then suddenly Mrs. Penarth had turned and shot out her finger at her. "You silly tipsy old crone," she had cried. "Down on your knees and crave my pardon, and then get home and don't cross my way again."

Sure enough Sally knelt on the stones, and slunk off home, and thereafter, if Mrs. Penarth was down in the village, she would make haste to get into her cottage, and shut the door. Mrs. Penarth, it seemed, knew more than Sally.

Judith swung her easy way up the steep hill, hatless in spite of the hot sun, and unbreathed by the ascent. She was a tall woman, black-haired and comely, her skin clear and healthy with the bloom on it that only sun and air can give. Her full-lipped mouth hinted that passion smoldered there; her eyebrows, fine and level, nearly met across the base of her forehead; her eyes, big and black, looked ever so slightly inwards. So small was the convergence that it was no disfigurement: when she looked directly at you it was not perceptible, but if she was immersed in her own thoughts, then it was there. Most noticeable was it when her father was dictating to her some grim story of malign magic or witchcraft. . . . But now she had come to the paved path through the garden of the farmhouse set with flowers and herbs in front of the espaliered apple trees, and there was Mrs. Penarth, knitting in the shade of the house during these hot hours before she went out again to chicken run and milking shed.

"Eh, but you're a welcome sight, Miss Judith," she said in the soft Cornish speech. "And you hatless in the sun, as ever, but indeed you're one of the wise who have made sun and rain their friends, and 'tis far you'd have to search ere you found better. Come in, dear soul, and have a glass of currant water after your walk, and tell me the doings down to St. Gervase."

Judith always fell into their mode of speech when she was with the native folk.

"Sure, there's little to tell," she said. "There was a grand catch two days agone, and yesterday was the burying of old Sally Trenair."

Mrs. Penarth poured out for her a glass of the clear ruby liquor for which she was famous.

"Strange how the folk were scared of that tipsy old poppet," she said. "She had nobbut a few rhymes to gabble and a foul tongue to flap at them. A tale of curses she blew off at me one day, and I doubt not she hid my name in the wishing well, though I never troubled to look."

"Hid your name in the wishing well?" asked Judith, thinking of the morning's dictation.

Mrs. Penarth shot a swift oblique glance at her. There were certain things she had noticed about Judith, and they interested her.

"Aw, my dear, you've sure got too much sense and book learning to heed such tales," she said. "But when I was a girl my mother used to talk of them. Even now I scarce know what to make of such strange things."

"Oh, tell me of them," said Judith. "My father's just set on the wishing wells and the lore of them. He was dictating to me of them all the morning."

"Eh, to think of that! Well, when I was a girl there were a many queer doings round the well. A maid would tell an old crone like Sally if she fancied a young man, and get some gabble to con over as she sipped the water. Or if a fellow had an ill will towards another he'd consult a witch-woman and she'd write the name of his enemy for him, and bid him hide it in the well. And then, sure as eve or morning, tribulations drove fast on him, as long as his name bided there. His cows would go dry or his boat be wrecked or his children get deadly dwalms or his wife break her marriage vows. Or he himself would pine and fail till he was scarce able to put foot to floor, and presently the bell would be tolling for him. Idle tales no doubt."

Judith had been drinking this in, eager as the thirsty earth drinks the rain after drought or as a starving man sets his teeth to food. Her mouth smiled, her blood beat high and strong; it was as if she was learning some news of good fortune which was hers by birthright. Just then there came a step in the passage and the door opened.

"Why, 'tis Steven," said Mrs. Penarth. "Come, lad, and pay your duty to Miss Judith, maybe she remembers you."

Tall as she was, he towered over her: he had a boy's face still, and the sea was in his eyes and the sun in his hair. And on the instant Judith knew that no magnet of man would avail to draw her from St. Gervase.

There was dictation again for her up till suppertime, and when, after that, her father went back to his books, she strolled out, as she often did on hot nights like this, before going to bed. Never yet had she felt so strong an emotional excitement as that afternoon when Mrs. Penarth, talking of those old beliefs of her girlhood, had somehow revealed Judith to herself. All that narrative about the wishing well was already familiar to some secret cell in her brain: she needed only to be reminded of it to make it her own. On the top of that had come Steven's entry, and her heart had leaped to him. Some mixed brew of these two was at ferment within her now; sometimes a bubble from one, sometimes from the other rose luminous to the surface. She felt restless and tingling with stored energy, and she paused for a moment at the gate of the garden, uncertain how to spend it.

The night was thickly overcast, the road that led down the village a riband of gray, scarcely visible, and as she stood there she heard a step brisk and active coming along it, and there swung into view, recognizable even in the deep dusk by his height and gait, the figure of Steven on his way to the village. Dearly would she have loved to call to him and walk with him, but that could not be: besides another desire tugged at her, and when he was past, she turned in at the lich gate to the churchyard. The white tombstones glimmered faintly in the dusk, and she looked up beyond them towards the grave by which she had stood two days ago at the burying of old Sally. Then her breath caught in her throat, for she could see the mound of new-turned earth gleaming whitely. She made her way to it: this dark earth was certainly luminous with some wavering light, and on the moment she was conscious that Sally herself, not the mere bag of bones that had been put away in the earth, was close to her. So vivid was this impression that she whispered, "Sally! Are you here, Sally?" No audible response came, but the answer tingled in every nerve in her body, and she knew that Sally was here, no pale wandering spirit, but a power friendly and sisterly and altogether evil. It was trickling into her, growing warm in her veins, as by some transfusion of blood. She went to the wishing well and, kneeling on the curbstone of it, drank of its water from her cupped hands.

Something stirred beside her, and turning, she saw at her side, illuminated by some pale gleam, a little bent figure shrouded in clean graveclothes and the brown wizened face, which she had last beheld in the composure and dignity of death, now all alive with glee and with welcome. And her flesh was weak, for in a spasm of terror she sprang to her feet with arms flung out against the specter, and lo, there was nothing there but the quiet churchyard with the headstones of those who slumbered there, and at her feet the black invisible water of which she had drunk. Despising herself for the fright, and yet winged with it, she ran stumbling from the place, not halting till she was back at the vicarage, where the light shining from the library window showed that her father was still pursuing his academic researches into the world of things occult and terrible of which the doors were now swinging open to admit her in very truth.

For some days the horror of that moment by the well was effective, and she threw herself into the normal ways of life which lured her with a new brightness. She often saw Steven, for it was he who brought the milk of a morning from the farm, and she would be out in the garden by the time of his early arrival cutting roses for her vases or more strenuously engaged in weeding the borders. At first she gave him just a nodded "good morning," but soon they would stand chatting there for five minutes. She knew she made a fine handsome figure; she saw he appreciated her healthy splendor; he looked at her with the involuntary tribute a man pays to a good-looking woman. Fond, wild notions took root in her mind, spreading their fibers beneath in the soil, and anchoring there. . . . Another morning she heard him singing as he clattered down the road in the milk cart, a big rough resonant voice of a high pitch for a man. Judith played the organ in church, conducting a choir practice every Saturday for the singers, and next week Steven was sitting among the men while she took them through the canticles and hymns. Women and girls took alto and treble parts; the chief chorister was Nance Pascoe, a maid of twenty, and she was like a folded rosebud just bursting into full flower. By some blind instinct Judith began to dislike her: she would stop in the middle of a verse to tell the trebles they were flat, which meant that Nance was the culprit. Again she would ask the tenors singly to sing some line over which they had bungled, and had a word of praise for Steven. Or she would go to the farm for a chat with Mrs. Penarth, and by some casual questions learn that Steven was hedge-clipping nearby in the meadow. Then she would remember she wanted a chicken for next day, and go to tell him: it was but a step. In a hundred infinitesimal ways she betrayed herself.

Mixed with this growth of longing which had so firmly rooted itself was another of more poisonous breed. There was a power eager to help her, and like a frightened fool she had fled from its manifestation. But she knew she was making no way with Steven, and now she bethought herself again of it, and found that her terror had withered, and that her thirst for commerce with those dark enchantments was keen not only for the help they could give her, but for her own love of them. Once more in the evening, when her father was back at his books, she set out for the wishing well.

Her step was noiseless on the grass of the church-yard, and she was close to the wishing well, still screened by bushes that grew there, when she heard from behind them a ringing man's laugh, and a girl's voice joined in.

"Sure, she's terrible set on you, Steven. It makes me bubble within when she says at the choir-singing, 'Yes, very nice, Mr. Penarth,' and what the poor soul means is 'Aw, Steven, doo'ee come and give me a hug.' "

Steven laughed again.

"I'm fair scared of her," he said, "though mother laughs fit to burst when she's come up to the farm to see and order one egg or a sprig of mint. And every morning when I take the milk the old girl'll be weeding and hoeing, showing-off like, as if she was the strong man at the fair."

"Eh, I declare I'm sorry for her," said Nance, "for I know what it is to love you. Poor empty heart!"

"Nance, we must put our banns up," said he. "I'm scared, but give your lad a kiss to strengthen him, and I'll pluck up and ask Parson to read us out next Sunday."

There was silence.

"Eh, Steven, don't hug so tight," whispered Nance. "You'll get your fill of me ere long. Just a drink from the well for us both, and then I must get home."

Judith stole back along the grass and from behind the curtain in the parlor window saw the two, arm-entwined, pass down the road. No thought was there now in her mind of any love philter, no longer did she want the help of a friendly power to get Steven. He had mocked at her, he was scared of her, and soon he would have good reason for that. Of Nance she hardly thought: it was not for Nance that her heart was black as the water in the wishing well. . . . She felt no hysterical rage or longing for revenge; it was a hellish glee that fed her soul. Quaint and pleasant was it, she thought, as she wrote on a slip of paper the name of Steven Penarth, that it should have been his mother who had taught her that. Mrs. Penarth had laughed "fit to burst" at her, so Mrs. Penarth must learn not to laugh so much.

She went forth with the inscribed slip. The power she courted was flooding into her, wave on wave. Now she was back at the well again, and there she knelt a moment drinking in like a thirsty field the dew of power with which the air was thick. She felt in the darkness for one of those fern-fringed niches in the wall, and deep among its fronds she hid the paper.

"Master of evil and of me," she muttered, "send sickness and death on him whom I here dedicate."

Something stirred beside her: she knew that the presence which had terrified her before was manifest again. She turned with hands of welcome, and there beside her was the shroud-wrapped figure and the wizened face, but now the shroud was white no longer but spotted with earth-mold, and the flesh was rotting from the face. Judith put her arms close round the specter, and kissed the frayed lips fretted with decay, and she felt it melting into her. She shut her eyes in the ecstasy of that union; when she opened them she was clasping the empty air.

She was down early next morning, full of youthful fire and fitness, and presently the milk cart clattered up to the gate. But it was not Steven who drove it, but Mrs. Penarth.

" 'Tis I who've come with your milk today, Miss Judith," she said, "for Steven's got a terrible bad headache, and I bade him lie abed. But he charged me to ask Parson to put up his banns, come Sunday."

"Oh, is Mr. Steven to be married?" asked Judith. "Who's the maid?"

"Just Nance Pascoe whom he's played with since he was a lad."

"Then he's lucky," said Judith, "for she's pretty as a picture. I'll tell my father about the banns. And I'm so sorry Mr. Steven's not well. But he'll mend quick."

The days passed on, and soon it was seen that Steven lay stricken with some sore fever to which neither his mother's healing hands nor the doctor's potions brought relief. Every morning Judith learned from Mrs. Penarth that he was no better, and every morning she felt herself the object of some keen, silent scrutiny. She was not one who prinked before her glass, but one day after Mrs. Penarth had gone, she ran upstairs and questioned her face. It certainly had changed: it was sharper in outline, and that cast in her eye was surely more pronounced. But she liked that: it seemed an outward and visible sign of her power. Every night now she sat by the wishing well concentrating on her desire. The news of Steven had been joyfully bad that day: his fever had burned more fiercely, consuming the flesh on his bones and drinking up his strength. Twice now had his banns been called, but it was not likely that he would go to church as a bridegroom.

The moon was soon to rise as Judith got up to go home: she fancied she heard something stir in the bushes by the well, and called, "Sally, Sally," but no response came. Her limbs were light with joy, she danced along the strip of turf leaping high in the air for the very exuberance of her soul. . . . As soon as she turned out of the gate Mrs. Penarth stole out of the bushes. She had a dark lantern with her, and she searched the walls of the wishing well. She spied the paper Judith had hidden there, and she drew it out and read it. She tore it in half, and on the blank piece she wrote another name, and put it back exactly where it had been. That night Steven slept well and long, and in the morning, even as Judith had surmised, he was "mending quick."

Judith was not in the garden at the milk hour to hear the favorable report, and later in the day Dr. Addis was called in: he found her suffering from just such an attack of fever as he had been attending for the past fortnight. It puzzled him, but his treatment of the other patient was proving successful, and he assured her father there was no cause for alarm: fevers ran their course. And Judith's fever ran its course even more fiercely.

She was lying in her bed facing the window ten

days after she had been taken ill. She knew that the power she had absorbed into her when she embraced that spectral horror by the wishing well was being drained out of her by some vaster potency, which, vampirelike, was drinking up her own vitality as well. She had been quite conscious all day, but often she had seen, waveringly, like the flame of a candle blown this way and that in the draft, the dim semblance of that shrouded figure round which she had cast her welcoming arms. It seemed to be still attached to her by some band of filmy whiteness and to be incomplete, but about the hour of sunset she saw that the specter stood by her bed, fully formed and severed from her. The face was now deeply pitted by corruption, and it floated away from her and drifted out the window. She was left here, human once more, but sick unto death.

She remembered how she had written Steven's name, and dedicated him to the power of the wishing well. Yet what had come of that? For the last week now Steven had brought the morning's milk, hale and handsome, with inquiries about her from his mother.

Could it be, she questioned herself, that she had failed in some point of the damnable ritual, and that what she had written was active not for his doom but for hers? It would be wise to destroy that slip of paper, if she could only get to it, not because she had ceased to wish him evil, but from the fear that it was her vitality that was being drained from her on that fruitless purpose.

She got out of bed, giddy with weakness, and

managed to get into a skirt and jersey, and slip her feet into her shoes. The house was quiet and step by step she struggled downstairs and to the door. The wholesome wind off the sea put a little life into her, and she shuffled along the strip of turf down which she had danced and capered and which lay between the lich gate and the well. She passed round the screen of bushes, and there on the stone bench was Steven's mother. She rose as Judith appeared and curtsied.

"Aw, dear. Why, you look poorly indeed, Miss Judith," she said. "Is it wise for you to come out? To the wishing well, too; there have been strange doings here."

"Oh, I'll be mending soon," said Judith. "A drink from the wishing well was what I fancied."

She knelt down on the curb, leaning one hand against the wall of the well, while with the other she felt among the ferns that fringed it. There was the slip of paper she had hidden, and she drew it forth.

"Take your drink then, Miss Judith," said Mrs. Penarth. "Why, whatever have you found? That's a queer thing to have gotten! A slip of paper is it? Open it, dear soul: maybe there's some good news in it."

Judith crushed it up in her hand; there was no need for her to look, and even as she knelt there, she felt a sweet lightening and cooling of her fever come over her.

Mrs. Penarth shot out her hand at her.

"Open it, you slut, you paltry witch," she screamed. "Do my bidding!"

Judith opened it, and read her own name written there.

She tried to rise to her feet; she swayed and staggered and she fell forward into the wishing well. It was very deep, and the sides of it were slippery with slime and water moss. Once she caught at the step on which she had knelt, but her fingers failed to grasp it, and she sank. Once after that she rose and then there came a roaring in her ears, and to her eyes a blackness, and down her throat there poured the cool water of the wishing well.

That Hell-Bound Train

ROBERT BLOCH

When Martin was a little boy, his daddy was a railroad man. Daddy never rode the high iron, but he walked the tracks for the CB&Q, and he was proud of his job. And every night when he got drunk, he sang this old song about "That Hell-Bound Train."

Martin didn't quite remember any of the words, but he couldn't forget the way his daddy sang them out. And when Daddy made the mistake of getting drunk in the afternoon and got squeezed between a Pennsy tank car and an AT&SF gondola, Martin sort of wondered why the Brotherhood didn't sing the song at his funeral.

After that, things didn't go so good for Martin, but somehow he always recalled Daddy's song. When Mom up and ran off with a traveling salesman from Keokuk (Daddy must have turned over in his grave, knowing she'd done such a thing, and with a *passenger*, too!), Martin hummed the tune to himself every night in the Orphan Home. And after Martin himself ran away, he used to whistle the song softly at night in the jungles, after the other bindlestiffs were asleep.

Martin was on the road for four or five years before he realized he wasn't getting anyplace. Of course, he'd tried his hand at a lot of things—picking fruit in Oregon, washing dishes in a Montana hash house, stealing hubcaps in Denver and tires in Oklahoma City—but by the time he'd put in six months on the chain gang down in Alabama he knew he had no future drifting around this way on his own.

So he tried to get on the railroad like his daddy had, and they told him that times were bad.

But Martin couldn't keep away from the railroads. Wherever he traveled, he rode the rods; he'd rather hop a freight heading north in sub-zero weather than lift his thumb to hitch a ride with a Cadillac headed for Florida. Whenever he managed to get hold of a can of Sterno, he'd sit there under a nice warm culvert, think about the old days, and often as not he'd hum the song about "That Hell-Bound Train." That was the train the drunks and the sinners rode—the gambling men and the grifters, the big-time spenders, the skirt chasers, and all the jolly crew. It would be really fine to take a trip in such good company, but Martin didn't like to think of what happened when that train finally pulled into the Depot Way Down Yonder. He didn't figure on spending eternity stoking the boilers in hell, without even a company union to protect him.

Still, it would be a lovely ride. If there *was* such a thing as a hell-bound train. Which, of course, there wasn't.

At least Martin didn't *think* there was, until that evening when he found himself walking the tracks heading south, just outside of Appleton Junction. The night was cold and dark, the way November nights are in the Fox River Valley, and he knew he'd have to work his way down to New Orleans for the winter, or maybe even Texas. Somehow he didn't much feel like going, even though he'd heard tell that a lot of those Texas automobiles had solid-gold hubcaps.

No sir, he just wasn't cut out for petty larceny. It was worse than a sin—it was unprofitable, too. Bad enough to do the devil's work, but then to get such miserable pay on top of it! Maybe he'd better let the Salvation Army convert him.

Martin trudged along humming Daddy's song, waiting for a rattler to pull out of the Junction behind him. He'd have to catch it—there was nothing else for him to do.

But the first train to come along came from the other direction, roaring toward him along the track from the south.

Martin peered ahead, but his eyes couldn't match his ears, and so far all he could recognize was the sound. It *was* a train, though; he felt the steel shudder and sing beneath his feet.

And yet, how could it be? The next station south was Neenah-Menasha, and there was nothing due out of there for hours.

The clouds were thick overhead, and the field mists rolled like a cold fog in a November midnight. Even so, Martin should have been able to see the headlight as the train rushed on. But there was only the whistle, screaming out of the black throat of the night. Martin could recognize the equipment of just about any locomotive ever built, but he'd never heard a whistle that sounded like this one. It wasn't signaling; it was screaming like a lost soul.

He stepped to one side, for the train was almost on top of him now. And suddenly there it was, looming along the tracks and grinding to a stop in less time than he'd believed possible. The wheels hadn't been oiled, because they screamed too, screamed like the damned. But the train slid to a halt, and the screams died away into a series of low, groaning sounds, and Martin looked up and saw that this was a passenger train. It was big and black, without a single light shining in the engine cab or any of the long string of cars; Martin couldn't read any lettering on the sides, but he was pretty sure this train didn't belong on the Northwestern Road.

He was even more sure when he saw the man clamber down out of the forward car. There was something wrong about the way he walked, as though one of his feet dragged, and about the lantern he carried. The lantern was dark, and the man held it up to his mouth and blew, and instantly it glowed redly. You don't have to be a member of the Railway Brotherhood to know that this is a mighty peculiar way of lighting a lantern.

As the figure approached, Martin recognized the

conductor's cap perched on his head, and this made him feel a little better for a moment—until he noticed that it was worn a bit too high, as though there might be something sticking up on the forehead underneath it.

Still, Martin knew his manners, and when the man smiled at him, he said, "Good evening, Mr. Conductor."

"Good evening, Martin."

"How did you know my name?"

The man shrugged. "How did you know I was the conductor?"

"You are, aren't you?"

"To you, yes. Although other people, in other walks of life, may recognize me in different roles. For instance, you ought to see what I look like to the folks out in Hollywood." The man grinned. "I travel a great deal," he explained.

"What brings you here?" Martin asked.

"Why, you ought to know the answer to that, Martin. I came because you needed me. Tonight, I suddenly realized you were backsliding. Thinking of joining the Salvation Army, weren't you?"

"Well—" Martin hesitated.

"Don't be ashamed. To err is human, as somebody-or-other once said. *Reader's Digest*, wasn't it? Never mind. The point is, I felt you needed me. So I switched over and came your way."

"What for?"

"Why, to offer you a ride, of course. Isn't it better to travel comfortably by train than to march along the cold streets behind a Salvation Army band? Hard on the feet, they tell me, and even harder on the eardrums."

"I'm not sure I'd care to ride your train, sir," Martin said. "Considering where I'm likely to end up."

"Ah, yes. The old argument." The Conductor sighed. "I suppose you'd prefer some sort of bargain, is that it?"

"Exactly," Martin answered.

"Well, I'm afraid I'm all through with that sort of thing. There's no shortage of prospective passengers anymore. Why should I offer you any special inducements?"

"You must want me, or else you wouldn't have bothered to go out of your way to find me."

The Conductor sighed again. "There you have a point. Pride was always my besetting weakness, I admit. And somehow I'd hate to lose you to the competition, after thinking of you as my own all these years." He hesitated. "Yes, I'm prepared to deal with you on your own terms, if you insist."

"The terms?" Martin asked.

"Standard proposition. Anything you want."

"Ah," said Martin.

"But I warn you in advance, there'll be no tricks. I'll grant you any wish you can name—but in return, you must promise to ride the train when the time comes."

"Suppose it never comes?"

"It will."

"Suppose I've got the kind of wish that will keep me off forever?"

"There is no such wish."

"Don't be too sure."

"Let me worry about that," the Conductor told him. "No matter what you have in mind, I warn you that I'll collect in the end. And there'll be none of this last-minute hocus-pocus, either. No last-hour repentances, no blonde *fräuleins* or fancy lawyers showing up to get you off. I offer a clean deal. That is to say, you'll get what you want, and I'll get what I want."

"I've heard you trick people. They say you're worse than a used-car salesman."

"Now wait a minute—"

"I apologize," Martin said hastily. "But it *is* supposed to be a fact that you can't be trusted."

"I admit it. On the other hand, you seem to think you have found a way out."

"A sure-fire proposition."

"Sure-fire? Very funny!" The man began to chuckle, then halted. "But we waste valuable time, Martin. Let's get down to cases. What do you want from me?"

Martin took a deep breath. "I want to be able to stop time."

"Right now?"

"No. Not yet. And not for everybody. I realize that would be impossible, of course. But I want to be able to stop time for myself. Just once in the future. Whenever I get to a point where I know I'm happy and contented, that's where I'd like to stop. So I can just keep on being happy forever."

"That's quite a proposition," the Conductor mused.

"I've got to admit I've never heard anything just like it before—and believe me, I've listened to some lulus in my day." He grinned at Martin. "You've really been thinking about this, haven't you?"

"For years," Martin admitted. Then he coughed. "Well, what do you say?"

"It's not impossible, in terms of your own *subjective* time sense," the Conductor murmured. "Yes, I think it could be arranged."

"But I mean *really* to stop. Not for me just to *imagine* it."

"I understand. And it can be done."

"Then you'll agree?"

"Why not? I promised you, didn't I? Give me your hand."

Martin hesitated. "Will it hurt very much? I mean, I don't like the sight of blood and—"

"Nonsense! You've been listening to a lot of poppycock. We already have made our bargain, my boy. I merely intend to put something into your hand. The ways and means of fulfilling your wish. After all, there's no telling at just what moment you may decide to exercise the agreement, and I can't drop everything and come running. So it's better if you can regulate matters for yourself."

"You're going to give me a time stopper?"

"That's the general idea. As soon as I can decide what would be practical." The Conductor hesitated. "Ah, the very thing! Here, take my watch."

He pulled it out of his vest pocket: a railroad watch in a silver case. He opened the back and made a delicate adjustment; Martin tried to see just exactly what he was doing, but the fingers moved in a blinding blur.

"There we are," the Conductor smiled. "It's all set, now. When you finally decide where you'd like to call a halt, merely turn the stem in reverse and unwind the watch until it stops. When it stops, time stops, for you. Simple enough?" And the Conductor dropped the watch into Martin's hand.

The young man closed his fingers tightly around the case. "That's all there is to it, eh?"

"Absolutely. But remember—you can stop the watch only once. So you'd better make sure that you're satisfied with the moment you choose to prolong. I caution you in all fairness; make very certain of your choice."

"I will." Martin grinned. "And since you've been so fair about it, I'll be fair, too. There's one thing you seem to have forgotten. It doesn't really matter *what* moment I choose. Because once I stop time for myself, that means I stay where I am forever. I'll never have to get older. And if I don't get any older, I'll never die. And if I never die, then I'll never have to take a ride on your train."

The Conductor turned away. His shoulders shook convulsively, and he may have been crying. "And you said *I* was worse than a used-car salesman," he gasped, in a strangled voice.

Then he wandered off into the fog, and the train whistle gave an impatient shriek, and all at once it was moving swiftly down the track, rumbling out of sight in the darkness.

Martin stood there, blinking down at the silver

watch in his hand. If it wasn't that he could actually see it and feel it there, and if he couldn't smell that peculiar odor, he might have thought he'd imagined the whole thing from start to finish—train, Conductor, bargain, and all.

But he had the watch, and he could recognize the scent left by the train as it departed, even though there aren't many locomotives around that use sulfur and brimstone as fuel.

And he had no doubts about his bargain. That's what came of thinking things through to a logical conclusion. Some fools would have settled for wealth, or power, or Kim Novak. Daddy might have sold out for a fifth of whiskey.

Martin knew that he'd made a better deal. Better? It was foolproof. All he needed to do now was choose his moment.

He put the watch in his pocket and started back down the railroad track. He hadn't really had a destination in mind before, but he did now. He was going to find a moment of happiness. . . .

Now young Martin wasn't altogether a ninny. He realized perfectly well that happiness is a relative thing; there are conditions and degrees of contentment, and they vary with one's lot in life. As a hobo, he was often satisfied with a warm handout, a double-length bench in the park, or a can of Sterno made in 1957 (a vintage year). Many a time he had reached a state of momentary bliss through such simple agencies, but he was aware that there were better things. Martin determined to seek them out.

Within two days he was in the great city of Chicago. Quite naturally, he drifted over to West Madison Street, and there he took steps to elevate his role in life. He became a city bum, a panhandler, a moocher. Within a week he had risen to the point where happiness was a meal in a regular one-arm luncheon joint, a two-bit flop on a real army cot in a real flophouse, and a full fifth of muscatel.

There was a night, after enjoying all three of these luxuries to the full, when Martin thought of unwinding his watch at the pinnacle of intoxication. But he also thought of the faces of the honest johns he'd braced for a handout today. Sure, they were squares, but they were prosperous. They wore good clothes, held good jobs, drove nice cars. And for them, happiness was even more ecstatic—they ate dinner in fine hotels, they slept on innerspring mattresses, they drank blended whiskey.

Squares or no, they had something there. Martin fingered his watch, put aside the temptation to hock it for another bottle of muscatel, and went to sleep determined to get himself a job and improve his happiness quotient.

When he awoke he had a hangover, but the determination was still with him. Before the month was out Martin was working for a general contractor over on the South Side, at one of the big rehabilitation projects. He hated the grind, but the pay was good, and pretty soon he got himself a one-room apartment out on Blue Island Avenue. He was accustomed to eating in decent restaurants now, and he bought himself a comfortable bed, and every

Saturday night he went down to the corner tavern. It was all very pleasant, but—

The foreman liked his work and promised him a raise in a month. If he waited around, the raise would mean that he could afford a second-hand car. With a car, he could even start picking up a gal for a date now and then. Other fellows on the job did, and they seemed pretty happy.

So Martin kept on working, and the raise came through and the car came through and pretty soon a couple of girls came through.

The first time it happened, he wanted to unwind his watch immediately. Until he got to thinking about what some of the older men always said. There was a guy named Charlie, for example, who worked alongside him on the hoist. "When you're young and don't know the score, maybe you get a kick out of running around with those pigs. But after a while, you want something better. A nice girl of your own. That's the ticket."

Martin felt he owed it to himself to find out. If he didn't like it better, he could always go back to what he had.

Almost six months went by before Martin met Lillian Gillis. By that time he'd had another promotion and was working inside, in the office. They made him go to night school to learn how to do simple bookkeeping, but it meant another fifteen bucks extra a week, and it was nicer working indoors.

And Lillian *was* a lot of fun. When she told him she'd marry him, Martin was almost sure that the time was now. Except that she was sort of—well, she was a *nice* girl, and she said they'd have to wait until they were married. Of course, Martin couldn't expect to marry her until he had a little more money saved up, and another raise would help, too.

That took a year. Martin was patient, because he knew it was going to be worth it. Every time he had any doubts, he took out his watch and looked at it. But he never showed it to Lillian, or anybody else. Most of the other men wore expensive wristwatches and the old silver railroad watch looked just a little cheap.

Martin smiled as he gazed at the stem. Just a few twists and he'd have something none of these other poor working slobs would ever have. Permanent satisfaction, with his blushing bride—

Only getting married turned out to be just the beginning. Sure, it was wonderful, but Lillian told him how much better things would be if they could move into a new place and fix it up. Martin wanted decent furniture, a TV set, a nice car.

So he started taking night courses and got a promotion to the front office. With the baby coming, he wanted to stick around and see his son arrive. And when it came, he realized he'd have to wait until it got a little older, started to walk and talk and develop a personality of its own.

About this time the company sent him out on the road as a troubleshooter on some of those other jobs, and now he *was* eating at those good hotels, living high on the hog and the expense account. More than once he was tempted to unwind his watch.

This was the good life. . . . Of course, it would be even better if he just didn't have to *work*. Sooner or later, if he could cut in on one of the company deals, he could make a pile and retire. Then everything would be ideal.

It happened, but it took time. Martin's son was going to high school before he really got up there into the chips. Martin got a strong hunch that it was now or never, because he wasn't exactly a kid anymore.

But right about then he met Sherry Westcott, and she didn't seem to think he was middle-aged at all, in spite of the way he was losing hair and adding stomach. She taught him that a toupee could cover the bald spot and a cummerbund could cover the pot gut. In fact, she taught him quite a lot and he so enjoyed learning that he actually took out his watch and prepared to unwind it.

Unfortunately, he chose the very moment that the private detectives broke down the door of the hotel room, and then there was a long stretch of time when Martin was so busy fighting the divorce action that he couldn't honestly say he was enjoying any given moment.

When he made the final settlement with Lil he was broke again, and Sherry didn't seem to think he was so young, after all. So he squared his shoulders and went back to work.

He made his pile eventually, but it took longer this time, and there wasn't much chance to have fun along the way. The fancy dames in the fancy cocktail lounges didn't seem to interest him anymore, and neither did the liquor. Besides, the Doc had warned him off that.

But there were other pleasures for a rich man to investigate. Travel, for instance—and not riding the rods from one hick burg to another, either. Martin went around the world by plane and luxury liner. For a while it seemed as though he would find his moment after all, visiting the Taj Mahal by moonlight. Martin pulled out the battered old watch case, and got ready to unwind it. Nobody else was there to watch him—

And that's why he hesitated. Sure, this was an enjoyable moment, but he was alone. Lil and the kid were gone, Sherry was gone, and somehow he'd never had time to make any friends. Maybe if he found new congenial people, he'd have the ultimate happiness. That must be the answer—it wasn't just money or power or sex or seeing beautiful things. The real satisfaction lay in friendship.

So on the boat trip home, Martin tried to strike up a few acquaintances at the ship's bar. But all these people were much younger, and Martin had nothing in common with them. Also they wanted to dance and drink and Martin wasn't in condition to appreciate such pastimes. Nevertheless, he tried.

Perhaps that's why he had the little accident the day before they docked in San Francisco. "Little accident" was the ship's doctor's way of describing it, but Martin noticed he looked very grave when he told him to stay in bed, and he'd called an ambulance to meet the liner at the dock and take the patient right to the hospital.

At the hospital, all the expensive treatment and the expensive smiles and the expensive words didn't fool Martin any. He was an old man with a bad heart, and they thought he was going to die.

But he could fool them. He still had the watch. He found it in his coat when he put on his clothes and sneaked out of the hospital.

He didn't have to die. He could cheat death with a single gesture—and he intended to do it as a free man, out there under a free sky.

That was the real secret of happiness. He understood it now. Not even friendship meant as much as freedom. This was the best thing of all—to be free of friends or family or the furies of the flesh.

Martin walked slowly beside the embankment under the night sky. Come to think of it, he was just about back where he'd started, so many years ago. But the moment was good, good enough to prolong forever. Once a bum, always a bum.

He smiled as he thought about it and then the smile twisted sharply and suddenly, like the pain twisting sharply and suddenly in his chest. The world began to spin, and he fell down on the side of the embankment.

He couldn't see very well, but he was still conscious, and he knew what had happened. Another stroke, and a bad one. Maybe this was it. Except that he wouldn't be a fool any longer. He wouldn't wait to see what was still around the corner.

Right now was his chance to use his power and save his life. And he was going to do it. He could still move; nothing could stop him.

He groped in his pocket and pulled out the old silver watch, fumbling with the stem. A few twists and he'd cheat death, he'd never have to ride that Hell-Bound Train. He could go on forever.

Forever.

Martin had never really considered the word before. To go on forever—but *how?* Did he *want* to go on forever, like this: a sick old man, lying helplessly here in the grass?

No. He couldn't do it. He wouldn't do it. And suddenly he wanted very much to cry, because he knew that somewhere along the line he'd outsmarted himself. And now it was too late. His eyes dimmed, there was a roaring in his ears. . . .

He recognized the roaring, of course, and he wasn't at all surprised to see the train come rushing out of the fog up there on the embankment. He wasn't surprised when it stopped, either, or when the Conductor climbed off and walked slowly toward him.

The Conductor hadn't changed a bit. Even his grin was still the same.

"Hello, Martin," he said. "All aboard."

"I know," Martin whispered. "But you'll have to carry me. I can't walk. I'm not even really talking anymore, am I?"

"Yes, you are," the Conductor said. "I can hear you fine. And you can walk, too." He leaned down and placed his hand on Martin's chest. There was a moment of icy numbness, and then, sure enough, Martin could walk after all.

He got up and followed the Conductor along

the slope, moving to the side of the train.

"In here?" he asked.

"No, the next car," the Conductor murmured. "I guess you're entitled to ride Pullman. After all, you're quite a successful man. You've tasted the joys of wealth and position and prestige. You've known the pleasures of marriage and fatherhood. You've sampled the delights of dining and drinking and debauchery, too, and you traveled high, wide, and handsome. So let's not have any last-minute recriminations."

"All right," Martin sighed. "I can't blame you for my mistakes. On the other hand, you can't take credit for what happened, either. I worked for everything I got. I did it all on my own. I didn't even need your watch."

"So you didn't," the Conductor said, smiling. "But would you mind giving it back to me now?"

"Need it for the next sucker, eh?" Martin muttered.

"Perhaps."

Something about the way he said it made Martin look up. He tried to see the Conductor's eyes, but the brim of the cap cast a shadow. So Martin looked down at the watch instead.

"Tell me something," he said softly. "If I give you the watch, what will you do with it?"

"Why, throw it into the ditch," the Conductor told him. "That's all I'll do with it." And he held out his hand.

"What if somebody comes along and finds it? And twists the stem backward, and stops time?"

"Nobody would do that," the Conductor murmured. "Even if they knew."

"You mean, it was all a trick? This is only an ordinary, cheap watch?"

"I didn't say that," whispered the Conductor. "I only said that no one has ever twisted the stem backward. They've all been like you, Martin—looking ahead to find that perfect happiness. Waiting for the moment that never comes."

The Conductor held out his hand again.

Martin sighed and shook his head. "You cheated me after all."

"You cheated yourself, Martin. And now you're going to ride that Hell-Bound Train."

He pushed Martin up the steps and into the car ahead. As he entered, the train began to move, and the whistle screamed. And Martin stood there in the swaying Pullman, gazing down the aisle at the other passengers. He could see them sitting there, and somehow it didn't seem strange at all.

Here they were: the drunks and the sinners, the gambling men and the grifters, the big-time spenders, the skirt chasers, and all the jolly crew. They knew where they were going, of course, but they didn't seem to give a damn. The blinds were drawn on the windows, yet it was light inside, and they were all living it up—singing and passing the bottle and roaring with laughter, throwing the dice and telling their jokes and bragging their big brags, just the way Daddy used to sing about them in the old song.

"Mighty nice traveling companions," Martin said.

"Why, I've never seen such a pleasant bunch of people. I mean, they seem to be really enjoying themselves!"

The Conductor shrugged. "I'm afraid things won't be quite so jazzy when we pull into that Depot Way Down Yonder."

For the third time, he held out his hand. "Now, before you sit down, if you'll just give me that watch. A bargain's a bargain—"

Martin smiled. "A bargain's a bargain," he echoed. "I agreed to ride your train if I could stop time when I found the right moment of happiness. And I think I'm about as happy right here as I've ever been."

Very slowly, Martin took hold of the silver watch stem.

"No!" gasped the Conductor. "No!"

But the watch stem turned.

"Do you realize what you've done?" the Conductor yelled. "Now we'll never reach the Depot! We'll just go on riding, all of us—forever!"

Martin grinned. "I know," he said. "But the fun is in the trip, not in the destination. You taught me that. And I'm looking forward to a wonderful trip. Look, maybe I can even help. If you were to find me another one of those caps, now, and let me keep this watch—"

And that's the way it finally worked out. Wearing his cap and carrying his battered old silver watch, there's no happier person in or out of this world—now and forever—than Martin. Martin, the new brakeman on that Hell-Bound Train.

As Gay As Cheese

JOAN AIKEN

Mr. Pol, the barber, always wore white overalls. He must have had at least six pairs, for every day he was snowy white and freshly starched as a marguerite, his blue eyes, red face, and bulbous nose appearing incongruously over the top of the bib. His shop looked like, and was, a kitchen, roughly adapted to barbering, with a mirror, basin, and some pictures of beautiful girls on the whitewashed walls. It was a long narrow crack of a room with the copper at one end and a tottering flight of steps at the other, leading down to the street; customers waiting their turn mostly sat on the steps in the sun, risking piles and reading *Men Only*.

Mr. Pol rented his upstairs room to an artist, and in the summertime when the customers had been shaved or trimmed, they sometimes went on up the stairs and bought a view of the harbor, water or oil, or a nice still life. The artist had an unlimited supply of these, which he whipped out with the dexterity of a card sharper.

Both men loved their professions. When the artist was not painting fourteen-by-ten-inch squares for the trippers, he was engaged on huge, complicated panels of mermaids, sharks, all mixed up with skulls, roses, and cabbages, while Mr. Pol hung over the heads of his customers as if he would have liked to gild them.

"Ah, I'm as gay as cheese this morning," he used to say, bustling into his kitchen with a long gnomish look at the first head of hair waiting to be shorn. "I'll smarten you up till you're like a new button mushroom."

"Now I'm as bright as a pearl," he would exclaim when the long rays of the early sun felt their way back to the copper with an underwater glimmer.

When Mr. Pol laid hands on a customer's head he knew more about that man than his mother did at birth, or his sweetheart or confessor—not only his past misdeeds, but his future ones, what he had had for breakfast and would have for supper, the name of his dog and the day of his death. This should have made Mr. Pol sad or cynical, but it did not. He remained impervious to his portentous gift. Perhaps this was because the destinies of the inhabitants of a small Cornish town contained nothing very startling, and Mr. Pol's divinings seldom soared higher or lower than a double twenty or a sprained ankle.

He never cut his own hair, and had no need to, for he was as bald as an egg.

"It was my own hair falling out that started me thinking on the matter," he told the artist. "All a man's nature comes out in the way hair grows. It's like a river—watch the currents and you can tell what it's come through, what sort of fish are in it, how fast it's running, how far to the sea."

The artist grunted. He was squatting on the floor, stretching a canvas, and made no reply. He was a taciturn man, who despised the trippers for buying his pink-and-green views.

Mr. Pol looked down at the top of his head and suddenly gave it an affectionate, rumpling pat, as one might to a large woolly dog.

"Ah, that's a nice head of hair. It's a shame you won't let me get at it."

"And have you knowing when I'm going to eat my last bite of bacon? Not likely."

"I wouldn't tell you, my handsome!" said Mr. Pol, very shocked. "I'm not one to go measuring people for their coffins before they're ready to step in. I'm as close as a false tooth. There's Sam now, off his lorry, the old ruin; I could tell a thing or two about him, but do I?"

He stumped off down the stairs, letting out a snatch of hymn in his powerful baritone.

"And there's some say," he went on, as he sculpted with his shears round the driver's wicked gray head, "that you can grow turnips from carrot seeds under the right moon. Who'd want to do that, I ask you?"

"Shorter round the ears," grumbled Sam, scowling down into the enamel basin.

* * * * *

When the night train from Paddington began to draw down the narrow valley towards the sea town, Brian and Fanny Dexter stood up stiffly from the seats where they had slept and started moving their luggage about. Brian was surly and silent, only remarking that it was damned cold and he hoped he could get a shave and a cup of coffee. Fanny glanced doubtfully at her reflection in the little greenish mirror. A white face and narrow eyes, brilliant from lack of sleep, glanced back at her.

"I'll be fine later," she said hopefully. Brian pulled on a sweater without comment. He looked rough but expensive, like a suede shoe. His thick light hair was beginning to gray, but hardly showed it.

"Lady Ward and Penelope said they'd be getting to Pengelly this week," Brian observed. "We might walk along the cliff path later on and see if they've arrived yet. We can do with some exercise to warm us and they'll be expecting us to call."

"I must do my shopping first. It's early closing, and there's all the food to lay in."

Brian shot her an angry look, and she was reminded that although the ice of their marriage seemed at the moment to be bearing, nevertheless there were frightening depths beneath and it was best not to loiter in doubtful spots.

"It won't take long," she said hurriedly.

"It was just an idea," Brian muttered, bundling up a camelhair overcoat. "Here we are, thank God."

It was still only nine in the morning. The town was gray and forbidding, tilted steeply down to a white sea. The fleet was out; the streets smelt of fish and emptiness. After they had had coffee Brian announced that he was going to get his shave.

"I'll do my shopping and meet you," suggested Fanny.

"No you bloody well won't, or you'll wander off for hours and I shall have to walk half over the town looking for you," snapped Brian. "You could do with a haircut yourself; you look like a Scotch terrier."

"All right."

She threaded her way after him between the empty tables of the café and across the road into Mr. Pol's shop. Mr. Pol was carefully rearranging his tattered magazines.

"Good morning, my handsome," he cautiously greeted Fanny's jeans and sweater and Eton crop, assessing her as a summer visitor.

"Can you give me a shave and my wife a haircut please?" cut in Brian briskly.

Mr. Pol looked from one to the other of them.

"I'll just put the kettle on for the shave, sir," he answered, moving leisurely to the inner room, "and then I'll trim the young lady, if you'd like to take a seat in the meanwhile."

Brian preferred to stroll back and lean against the doorpost with his hands in his pockets, while Mr. Pol wreathed Fanny's neck in a spotless towel. Her dark head, narrow as a boy's, was bent forward, and he looked benignly at the swirl of glossy hair, flicked a comb through it, and turned her head gently with the palms of his hands.

As he did so, a shudder like an electric shock ran through him and he started back, the comb between his thumb and forefinger jerking upward like a diviner's rod. Neither of the other two noticed; Brian was looking out into the street and Fanny had her eyes on her hands, which were locked together with white knuckles across a fold of the towel.

After a moment Mr. Pol gingerly replaced his palms on the sides of her head with a pretense of smoothing the downy hair above the ears, and again the shock ran through him. He looked into the mirror, almost expecting to see fish swimming and seaweed floating around her. Death by drowning, and so soon; he could smell salt water and see her thin arm stretch sideways in the wave.

"Don't waste too much time on her," said Brian, looking at his watch. "She doesn't mind what she looks like."

Fanny glanced up and met Mr. Pol's eyes in the glass. There was such a terrified appeal in her look that his hands closed instinctively on her shoulders and his lips shaped to form the words, "There, there, my handsome. Never mind," before he saw that her appeal was directed, not to him, but to her own reflection's pathetic power to please.

"That's lovely," she said to Mr. Pol with a faint smile, and stood up, shaking the glossy dark tufts off her. She sat on one of his chairs, looking at a magazine, while Brian took her place and Mr. Pol fetched his steaming kettle.

"You're visiting the town?" Mr. Pol asked as he

rubbed up the lather on his brush. He felt the need for talk.

"Just come off the night train; we're staying here, yes," Brian said curtly.

"It's a pretty place," Mr. Pol remarked. "Plenty of grand walks if you're young and active."

"We're going along to Pengelly by the cliff path this morning," said Brian.

"Oh, but I thought you only said we *might*—" Fanny began incautiously, and then bit off her words.

Brian shot her a look of such hatred that even Mr. Pol caught it, and scuttled into the next room for another razor.

"For Christ's sake, *will* you stop being so damned negative," Brian muttered to her furiously.

"But the groceries—"

"Oh, to hell with the groceries. We'll eat out. Lady Ward and Penelope will think it most peculiar if we don't call—they know we're here. I suppose you want to throw away a valuable social contact for the sake of a couple of ounces of tea. I can't think why you need to do this perpetual shopping—Penelope never does."

"I only thought—"

"Never mind what you thought."

Mr. Pol came back and finished the shave.

"That's a nice head of hair, sir," he said, running his hands over it professionally. "Do you want a trim at all?"

"No, thanks," replied Brian abruptly. "Chap in the Burlington Arcade always does it for me. Anything wrong?"

Mr. Pol was staring at the ceiling above Brian's head in a puzzled way.

"No—no, sir, nothing. Nothing at all. I thought for a moment I saw a bit of rope hanging down, but it must have been fancy." Nevertheless, Mr. Pol passed his hand once more above Brian's head with the gesture of someone brushing away cobwebs.

"Will that be all? Thank you, sir. Mind how you go on that path to Pengelly. 'Tis always slippery after the rain and we've had one or two falls of rock this summer; all this damp weather loosens them up."

"We'll be all right, thanks," said Brian, who had been walking out of the door without listening to what Mr. Pol was saying. "Come on, Fanny." He swung up the street with Fanny almost running behind him.

"Have they gone? Damnation, I thought I could sell them a view of the cliffs," said the artist, coming in with a little canvas. "Hullo, something the matter?"

For the barber was standing outside his door and staring in indecision and distress after the two figures, now just taking the turning up to the cliff path.

"No," he said at last, turning heavily back and picking up his broom. "No, I'm as gay as cheese."

And he began sweeping up the feathery tufts of dark hair from his stone floor.

Madame Mim

T. H. WHITE

The following selection is from the novel The Sword in the Stone, *T. H. White's fantasy about the boyhood of King Arthur. White's setting is a castle in legendary medieval England where young Arthur, called Wart, is a foster child. He lives with Sir Ector, the lord of the castle, and Ector's son, Kay, two years older than Wart. The boys' tutor is Merlyn, a powerful but kindly magician, and the only person who knows Wart's identity. The castle stands in a clearing of the Forest Sauvage, a sanctuary for wild beasts (among them, Kay's escaped hawk, Cully), a refuge for madmen and outlaws (including the noseless Wat), and a place of lurking evil.*

One Thursday afternoon the boys were doing their archery as usual. There were two straw targets fifty yards apart, and when they had shot their arrows at the one, they had only to go to it, collect them, and fire back at the other after facing about.

52

It was still the loveliest summer weather, and there had been chickens for dinner, so that Merlyn had gone off to the edge of their shooting-ground and sat down under a tree. What with the warmth and the chickens and the cream he had poured over his pudding and the continual repassing of the boys and the tock of the arrows in the targets—which was as sleepy to listen to as the noise of a lawn-mower—and the dance of the egg-shaped sunspots between the leaves of his tree, the aged magician was soon fast asleep.

Archery was a serious occupation in those days. It had not yet been relegated to Indians and small boys, so that when you were shooting badly you got into a bad temper, just as the wealthy pheasant shooters do today. Kay was shooting badly. He was trying too hard and plucking on his loose, instead of leaving it to the bow.

"Oh, come on," said Kay. "I'm sick of these beastly targets. Let's have a shot at the popinjay."

They left the targets and had several shots at the popinjay—which was a large, bright-colored arti-ficial bird stuck on the top of a stick, like a parrot—and Kay missed these also. First he had the feeling of "Well, I *will* hit the filthy thing, even if I have to go without my tea until I do it." Then he merely became bored.

The Wart said, "Let's play Rovers then. We can come back in half an hour and wake Merlyn up."

What they called Rovers consisted in going for a walk with their bows and shooting one arrow each at any agreed mark which they came across. Some-

times it would be a mole hill, sometimes a clump of
rushes, sometimes a big thistle almost at their feet.
They varied the distance at which they chose these
objects, sometimes picking a target as much as 120
yards away—which was about as far as these boys'
bows could carry—and sometimes having to aim
actually below a close thistle because the arrow always leaps up a foot or two as it leaves the bow.
They counted five for a hit, and one if the arrow
was within a bow's length, and added up their scores
at the end.

On this Thursday they chose their targets wisely,
and, besides, the grass of the big field had been
lately cut. So they never had to search for their
arrows for long, which nearly always happens, as
in golf, if you shoot ill-advisedly near hedges or in
rough places. The result was that they strayed further than usual and found themselves near the edge
of the savage forest where Cully had been lost.

"I vote," said Kay, "that we go to those buries in
the chase, and see if we can get a rabbit. It would
be more fun than shooting at these hummocks."

They did this. They chose two trees about a
hundred yards apart, and each boy stood under one
of them, waiting for the conies to come out again.
They stood very still, with their bows already raised
and arrows fitted, so that they would make the least
possible movement to disturb the creatures when
they did appear. It was not difficult for either of
them to stand thus, for the very first test which they
had had to pass in archery was standing with the
bow at arm's length for half an hour. They had six

arrows each and would be able to fire and mark them all before they needed to frighten the rabbits back by walking about to collect. An arrow does not make enough noise to upset more than the particular rabbit that it is shot at.

At the fifth shot Kay was lucky. He allowed just the right amount for wind and distance, and his point took a young coney square in the head. It had been standing up on end to look at him, wondering what he was.

"Oh, well shot!" cried the Wart as they ran to pick it up. It was the first rabbit they had ever hit, and luckily they had killed it dead.

When they had carefully gutted it with the little hunting knife which Merlyn had given—in order to keep it fresh—and passed one of its hind legs through the other at the hock, for convenience in carrying, the two boys prepared to go home with their prize. But before they unstrung their bows they used to observe a ceremony. Every Thursday afternoon, after the last serious arrow had been fired, they were allowed to fit one more nock to their strings and to discharge the arrow straight up into the air. It was partly a gesture of farewell, partly of triumph, and it was beautiful. They did it now as a salute to their first prey.

The Wart watched his arrow go up. The sun was already westing towards evening, and the trees where they were had plunged them into a partial shade. So, as the arrow topped the trees and climbed into sunlight, it began to burn against the evening like the sun itself. Up and up it went, not weaving as it would have done with a snatching loose, but soaring, swimming, aspiring towards heaven, steady, golden and superb. Just as it had spent its force, just as its ambition had been dimmed by destiny and it was preparing to faint, to turn over, to pour back into the bosom of its mother earth, a terrible portent happened. A gore-crow came flapping wearily before the approaching night. It came, it did not waver, it took the arrow. It flew away, heavy and hoisting, with the arrow in its beak.

Kay was frightened by this, but the Wart was furious. He had loved his arrow's movement, its burning ambition in the sunlight, and, besides, it was his best arrow. It was the only one which was perfectly balanced, sharp, tight-feathered, clean-nocked, and neither warped nor scraped.

"It was a witch," said Kay.

"I don't care if it was ten witches," said the Wart. "I am going to get it back."

"But it went towards the Forest."

"I shall go after it."

"You can go alone, then," said Kay. "I'm not going into the Forest Sauvage, just for a putrid arrow."

"I shall go alone."

"Oh, well," said Kay, "I suppose I shall have to come too, if you're so set on it. And I bet we shall get nobbled by Wat."

"Let him nobble," said the Wart. "I want my arrow."

They went in the Forest at the place where they had last seen the bird of carrion.

In less than five minutes they were in a clearing with a well and a cottage just like Merlyn's.

"Goodness," said Kay, "I never knew there were any cottages so close. I say, let's go back."

"I just want to look at this place," said the Wart. "It's probably a wizard's."

The cottage had a brass plate screwed on the garden gate. It said:

MADAME MIM, B.A. (Dom-Daniel)
PIANOFORTE
NEEDLEWORK
NECROMANCY
No Hawkers, circulars
or Income Tax.
Beware of the Dragon.

The cottage had lace curtains. These stirred ever so slightly, for behind them there was a lady peeping. The gore-crow was standing on the chimney.

"Come on," said Kay. "Oh, do come on. I tell you, she'll never give it us back."

At this point the door of the cottage opened suddenly and the witch was revealed standing in the passage. She was a strikingly beautiful woman of about thirty, with coal-black hair so rich that it had the blue-black of the maggot-pies in it, silky bright eyes, and a general soft air of butter-wouldn't-melt-in-my-mouth. She was sly.

"How do you do, my dears," said Madame Mim. "And what can I do for you today?"

The boys took off their leather caps, and Wart said, "Please, there is a crow sitting on your chimney and I think it has stolen one of my arrows."

"Precisely," said Madame Mim. "I have the arrow within."

"Could I have it back, please?"

"Inevitably," said Madame Mim. "The young gentleman shall have his arrow on the very instant, in four ticks and ere the bat squeaks thrice."

"Thank you very much," said the Wart.

"Step forward," said Madame Mim. "Honor the threshold. Accept the humble hospitality in the spirit in which it is given."

"I really do not think we can stay," said the Wart politely. "I really think we must go. We shall be expected back at home."

"Sweet expectation," replied Madame Mim in devout tones.

"Yet you would have thought," she added, "that the young gentlemen could have found time to honor a poor cottager, out of politeness. Few can believe how we ignoble tenants of the lower classes value a visit from the landlord's sons."

"We would like to come in," said the Wart, "very much. But you see we shall be late already."

The lady now began to give a sort of simpering whine. "The fare is lowly," she said. "No doubt it is not what you would be accustomed to eating, and so naturally such highly born ones would not care to partake."

Kay's strongly developed feeling for good form gave way at this. He was an aristocratic boy always, and condescended to his inferiors so that they could admire him. Even at the risk of visiting a witch, he was not going to have it said that he had refused to eat a tenant's food because it was too humble.

"Come on, Wart," he said. "We needn't be back before vespers."

Madame Mim swept them a low curtsey as they crossed the threshold. Then she took them each by the scruff of the neck, lifted them right off the ground with her strong gypsy arms, and shot out of the back door with them almost before they had got in at the front. The Wart caught a hurried glimpse of her parlor and kitchen. The lace curtains, the aspidistra, the lithograph called the Virgin's Choice, the printed text of the Lord's Prayer written backwards and hung upside down, the sea-shell, the needle-case in the shape of a heart with A Present from Camelot written on it, the broomsticks, the cauldrons, and the bottles of dandelion wine. Then they were kicking and struggling in the back yard.

"We thought that the growing sportsmen would care to examine our rabbits," said Madame Mim.

There was, indeed, a row of large rabbit hutches in front of them, but they were empty of rabbits. In one hutch there was a poor ragged old eagle owl, evidently quite miserable and neglected, in another a small boy unknown to them, a wittol who could only roll his eyes and burble when the witch came near. In a third there was a moulting black cock. A fourth had a mangy goat in it, also black, and two more stood empty.

"Grizzle Greediguts," cried the witch.

"Here, Mother," answered the carrion crow.

With a flop and a squawk it was sitting beside them, its hairy black beak cocked on one side. It was the witch's familiar.

"Open the doors," commanded Madame Mim, "and Greediguts shall have eyes for supper, round and blue."

The gore-crow hastened to obey, with every sign of satisfaction, and pulled back the heavy doors in its strong beak, with three times three. Then the two boys were thrust inside, one into each hutch, and Madame Mim regarded them with unmixed pleasure. The doors had magic locks on them and the witch had made them to open by whispering in their keyholes.

"As nice a brace of young gentlemen," said the witch, "as ever stewed or roast. Fattened on real butcher's meat, I daresay, with milk and all. Now we'll have the big one jugged for Sunday, if I can get a bit of wine to go in the pot, and the little one we'll have on the moon's morn, by jing and by jee, for how can I keep my sharp fork out of him a minute longer it fair gives me the croup."

"Let me out," said Kay hoarsely, "you old witch, or Sir Ector will come for you."

At this Madame Mim could no longer contain her joy. "Hark to the little varmint," she cried, snapping her fingers and doing a bouncing jig before the cages. "Hark to the sweet, audacious, tender little veal. He answers back and threatens us with Sir Ector, on the very brink of the pot. That's how I faint to tooth them, I do declare, and that's how I will tooth them ere the week be out by Scarmiglione, Belial, Peor, Ciriato Sannuto, and Dr. D."

With this she began bustling about in the back yard, the herb garden, and the scullery, cleaning pots, gathering plants for the stuffing, sharpening knives and cleavers, boiling water, skipping for joy, licking her greedy lips, saying spells, braiding her night-black hair, and singing as she worked.

First she sang the old witch's song:

> Black spirits and white, red spirits and gray,
> Mingle, mingle, mingle, you that mingle may.
>> Here's the blood of a bat,
>> Put in that, oh, put in that.
>> Here's libbard's bane.
>> Put in again.
> Mingle, mingle, mingle, you that mingle may.

Then she sang her work song:

> Two spoons of sherry
> Three oz. of yeast,
> Half a pound of unicorn,
> And God bless the feast.
> Shake them in a collander,
> Bang them to a chop,
> Simmer slightly, snip up nicely,
> Jump, skip, hop.
> Knit one, knot one, purl two together,
> Pip one and pop one and pluck the secret feather.
> Baste in a mod. oven.
> God bless our coven.

Tra-la-la!
Three toads in a jar.
Te-he-he!
Put in the frog's knee.
Peep out of the lace curtain.
There goes the Toplady girl, she's up to no
    good that's certain.
Oh, what a lovely baby!
How nice it would go with gravy.
Pinch the salt.

Here she pinched it very nastily.

Turn the malt.

Here she began twiddling round widdershins, in
a vulgar way.

With a hey-nonny-nonny and I don't mean
    maybe.

At the end of this song, Madame Mim took a
sentimental turn and delivered herself of several
hymns, of a blasphemous nature, and of a tender
love lyric which she sang sotto-voce with trills. It
was:

My love is like a red, red nose
His tail is soft and tawny,
And everywhere my lovely goes
I call him Nick or Horny.

* * * * *

She vanished into the parlor, to lay the table.

Poor Kay was weeping in a corner of the end hutch, lying on his face and paying no attention to anything. Before Madame Mim had finally thrown him in, she had pinched him all over to see if he was fat. She had also slapped him, to see, as the butchers put it, if he was hollow. On top of this, he did not in the least want to be eaten for Sunday dinner and he was miserably furious with the Wart for leading him into such a terrible doom on account of a mere arrow. He had forgotten that it was he who had insisted on entering the fatal cottage.

The Wart sat on his haunches, because the cage was too small for standing up, and examined his prison. The bars were of iron and the gate was iron too. He shook all the bars, one after the other, but they were as firm as rock. There was an iron bowl for water—with no water in it—and some old straw in a corner for lying down. It was verminous.

"Our mistress," said the mangy old goat suddenly from the next pen, "is not very careful of her pets."

He spoke in a low voice, so that nobody could hear, but the carrion crow which had been left on the chimney to spy upon them noticed that they were talking and moved nearer.

"Whisper," said the goat, "if you want to talk."

"Are you one of her familiars?" asked the Wart suspiciously.

The poor creature did not take offense at this, and tried not to look hurt.

"No," he said. "I'm not a familiar. I'm only a

mangy old black goat, rather tattered as you see, and kept for sacrifice."

"Will she eat you too?" asked the Wart, rather trembling.

"Not she. I shall be too rank for her sweet tooth, you may be sure. No, she will use my blood for making patterns with on Walpurgis Night.

"It's quite a long way off, you know," continued the goat without self-pity. "For myself I don't mind very much, for I am old. But look at the poor old owl there, that she keeps merely for a sense of possession and generally forgets to feed. That makes my blood boil, that does. It wants to fly, to stretch its wings. At night it just runs round and round and round like a big rat, it gets so restless. Look, it has broken all its soft feathers. For me, it doesn't matter, for I am naturally of a sedentary disposition now that youth has flown, but I call that owl a rare shame. Something ought to be done about it."

The Wart knew that he was probably going to be killed that night, the first to be released out of all that band, but yet he could not help feeling touched at the great-heartedness of this goat. Itself under sentence of death, it could afford to feel strongly about the owl. He wished he were as brave as this.

"If only I could get out," said the Wart. "I know a magician who would soon settle her hash, and rescue us all."

The goat thought about this for some time, nodding its gentle old head with the great cairngorm eyes. Then it said, "As a matter of fact I know how to get you out, only I did not like to mention it before. Put your ear nearer the bars. I know how to get you out, but not your poor friend there who is crying. I didn't like to subject you to a temptation like that. You see, when she whispers to the lock I have heard what she says, but only at the locks on either side of mine. When she gets a cage away she is too soft to be heard. I know the words to release both you and me, and the black cock here too, but not your young friend yonder."

"Why ever haven't you let yourself out before?" asked the Wart, his heart beginning to bound.

"I can't speak them in human speech, you see," said the goat sadly, "and this poor mad boy here, the wittol, he can't speak them either."

"Oh, tell them me."

"You will be safe then, and so would I and the cock be too, if you stayed long enough to let us out. But would you be brave enough to stay, or would you run at once? And what about your friend and the wittol and the old owl?"

"I should run for Merlyn at once," said the Wart. "Oh, at once, and he would come back and kill this old witch in two twos, and then we should all be out."

The goat looked at him deeply, his tired old eyes seeming to ask their way kindly into the bottom of his heart.

"I shall tell you only the words for your own lock," said the goat at last. "The cock and I will stay here with your friend, as hostages for your return."

"Oh, goat," whispered the Wart. "You could have made me say the words to get you out first and then gone your way. Or you could have got the three of us out, starting with yourself to make sure, and left Kay to be eaten. But you are staying with Kay. Oh, goat, I will never forget you, and if I do not get back in time I shall not be able to bear my life."

"We shall have to wait till dark. It will only be a few minutes now."

As the goat spoke, they could see Madame Mim lighting the oil lamp in the parlor. It had a pink glass shade with patterns on it. The crow, which could not see in the dark, came quietly closer, so that at least he ought to be able to hear.

"Goat," said the Wart, in whose heart something strange and terrible had been going on in the dangerous twilight, "put your head closer still. Please, goat, I am not trying to be better than you are, but I have a plan. I think it is I who had better stay as hostage and you had better go. You are black and will not be seen in the night. You have four legs and can run much faster than I. Let you go with a message for Merlyn. I will whisper you out, and I will stay."

He was hardly able to say the last sentence, for he knew that Madame Mim might come for him at any moment now, and if she came before Merlyn it would be his death warrant. But he did say it, pushing the words out as if he were breathing against water, for he knew that if he himself were gone when Madame came for him, she would certainly eat Kay at once.

"Master," said the goat without further words, and it put one leg out and laid its double-knobbed forehead on the ground in the salute which is given to royalty. Then it kissed his hand as a friend.

"Quick," said the Wart, "give me one of your hoofs through the bars and I will scratch a message on it with one of my arrows."

It was difficult to know what message to write on such a small space with such a clumsy implement. In the end he just wrote KAY. He did not use his own name because he thought Kay more important, and that they would come quicker for him.

"Do you know the way?" he asked.

"My grandam used to live at the castle."

"What are the words?"

"Mine," said the goat, "are rather upsetting."

"What are they?"

"Well," said the goat, "you must say: Let Good Digestion Wait on Appetite."

"Oh, goat," said the Wart in a broken voice. "How horrible. But run quickly, goat, and come back safely, goat, and oh, goat, give me one more kiss for company before you go." The goat refused to kiss him. It gave him the Emperor's salute, of both feet, and bounded away into the darkness as soon as he had said the words.

Unfortunately, although they had whispered too carefully for the crow to hear their speech, the release words had had to be said rather loudly to reach the next door keyhole, and the door had creaked.

"Mother, Mother!" screamed the crow. "The rabbits are escaping."

Instantly Madame Mim was framed in the lighted doorway of the kitchen.

"What is it, my Grizzle?" she cried. "What ails us, my halcyon tit?"

"The rabbits are escaping," shrieked the crow again.

The witch ran out, but too late to catch the goat or even to see him, and began examining the locks at once by the light of her fingers. She held these up in the air and a blue flame burned at the tip of each.

"One little boy safe," counted Madame Mim, "and sobbing for his dinner. Two little boys safe, and neither getting thinner. One mangy goat gone, and who cares a fiddle? For the owl and the cock are left, and the wittol in the middle.

"Still," added Madame Mim, "it's a caution how he got out, a proper caution, that it is."

"He was whispering to the little boy," sneaked the crow, "whispering for the last half-hour together."

"Indeed?" said the witch. "Whispering to the little dinner, hey? And much good may it do him. What about a sage stuffing, boy, hey? And what were you doing, my Greediguts, to let them carry on like that? No dinner for you, my little painted bird of paradise, so you may just flap off to any old tree and roost."

"Oh, Mother," whined the crow. "I was only adoing of my duty."

"Flap off," cried Madame Mim. "Flap off, and go broody if you like."

The poor crow hung its head and crept off to the other end of the roof, sneering to itself.

"Now, my juicy toothful," said the witch, turning to the Wart and opening his door with the proper whisper of Enough-Is-As-Good-As-a-Feast, "we think the cauldron simmers and the oven is mod. How will my tender suckling pig enjoy a little popping lard instead of the clandestine whisper?"

The Wart ran about in his cage as much as he could, and gave as much trouble as possible in being caught, in order to save even a little time for the coming of Merlyn.

"Let go of me, you beast," he cried. "Let go of me, you foul hag, or I'll bite your fingers."

"How the creature scratches," said Madame Mim. "Bless us, how he wriggles and kicks, just for being a pagan's dinner."

"Don't you dare kill me," cried the Wart, now hanging by one leg. "Don't you dare to lay a finger on me, or you'll be sorry for it."

"The lamb," said Madame Mim. "The partridge with a plump breast, how he does squeak.

"And then there's the cruel old custom," continued the witch, carrying him into the lamplight of the kitchen where a new sheet was laid on the floor, "of plucking a poor chicken before it is dead. The feathers come out cleaner so. Nobody could be so cruel as to do that nowadays, by Nothing or by Never, but of course a little boy doesn't feel any pain. Their clothes come off nicer if you take them off alive, and who would dream of roasting a little boy in his clothes, to spoil the feast?"

"Murderess," cried the Wart. "You will rue this ere the night is out."

"Cubling," said the witch. "It's a shame to kill him, that it is. Look how his little downy hair stares in the lamplight, and how his poor eyes pop out of his head. Greediguts will be sorry to miss those eyes, so she will. Sometimes one could almost be a vegetarian, when one has to do a deed like this."

The witch laid Wart over her lap, with his head between her knees, and carefully began to take his clothes off with a practiced hand. He kicked and squirmed as much as he could, reckoning that every hindrance would put off the time when he would be actually knocked on the head, and thus increase the time in which the black goat could bring Merlyn to his rescue. During this time the witch sang her plucking song, of:

> Pull the feather with the skin,
> Not against the grain—o.
> Pluck the soft ones out from in,
> The great with might and main—o.
> Even if he wriggles,
> Never heed his squiggles,
> For mercifully little boys are quite immune to
>   pain—o.

She varied this song with the other kitchen song of the happy cook:

> Soft skin for crackling,
> Oh, my lovely duckling,
> The skewers go here,

And the string goes there,
And such is my scrumptious suckling.

"You will be sorry for this," cried the Wart, "even
if you live to be a thousand."

"He has spoken enough," said Madame Mim. "It
is time that we knocked him on the napper."

Hold him by the legs, and
When up goes his head,
Clip him with the palm-edge, and
Then he is dead.

The dreadful witch now lifted the Wart into the
air and prepared to have her will of him; but at
that very moment there was a fizzle of summer
lightning without any crash and in the nick of time
Merlyn was standing on the threshold.

"Ha!" said Merlyn. "Now we shall see what a dou-
ble-first at Dom-Daniel avails against the private
education of my master Bleise."

Madame Mim put the Wart down without looking at him, rose from her chair, and drew herself
to her full magnificent height. Her glorious hair
began to crackle, and sparks shot out of her flashing
eyes. She and Merlyn stood facing each other a full
sixty seconds, without a word spoken, and then
Madame Mim swept a royal curtsey and Merlyn
bowed a frigid bow. He stood aside to let her go
first out of the doorway and then followed her into
the garden.

It ought perhaps to be explained, before we go any further, that in those far-off days, when there was actually a college for Witches and Warlocks under the sea at Dom-Daniel and when all wizards were either black or white, there was a good deal of ill-feeling between the different creeds. Quarrels between white and black were settled ceremonially, by means of duels. A wizard's duel was run like this. The two principals would stand opposite each other in some large space free from obstructions, and await the signal to begin. When the signal was given they were at liberty to turn themselves into things. It was rather like the game that can be played by two people with their fists. They say One, Two, Three and at Three they either stick out two fingers for scissors, or the flat palm for paper, or the clenched fist for stone. If your hand becomes paper when your opponent's becomes scissors, then he cuts you and wins; but if yours has turned into stone, his scissors are blunted, and the win is yours. The object of the wizard in the duel was to turn himself into some kind of animal, vegetable, or mineral which would destroy the particular animal, vegetable, or mineral which had been selected by his opponent. Sometimes it went on for hours.

Merlyn had Archimedes for his second, Madame Mim had the gore-crow for hers, while Hecate, who always had to be present at these affairs in order to keep them regular, sat on the top of a stepladder in the middle, to umpire. She was a cold, shining, muscular lady, the color of moonlight. Merlyn and Madame Mim rolled up their sleeves, gave their surcoats to Hecate to hold, and the latter put on a celluloid eye-shade to watch the battle.

At the first gong Madame Mim immediately turned herself into a dragon. It was the accepted opening move and Merlyn ought to have replied by being a thunderstorm or something like that. Instead, he caused a great deal of preliminary confusion by becoming a field mouse, which was quite invisible in the grass, and nibbled Madame Mim's tail, as she stared about in all directions, for about five minutes before she noticed him. But when she did notice the nibbling, she was a furious cat in two flicks.

Wart held his breath to see what the mouse would become next—he thought perhaps a tiger which could kill the cat—but Merlyn merely became another cat. He stood opposite her and made faces. This most irregular procedure put Madame Mim quite out of her stride, and it took her more than a minute to regain her bearings and become a dog. Even as she became it, Merlyn was another dog standing opposite her, of the same sort.

"Oh, well played, sir!" cried the Wart, beginning to see the plan.

Madame Mim was furious. She felt herself out of her depth against these unusual stone-walling tactics and experienced an internal struggle not to lose her temper. She knew that if she did lose it she would lose her judgment, and the battle as well. She did some quick thinking. If whenever she turned herself into a menacing animal, Merlyn was merely going to turn into the same kind, the thing would become either a mere dog-fight or stalemate. She had better alter her own tactics and give Merlyn a surprise.

At this moment the gong went for the end of the first round. The combatants retired into their respective corners and their seconds cooled them by flapping their wings, while Archimedes gave Merlyn a little massage by nibbling with his beak.

"Second round," commanded Hecate. "Seconds out of the ring. . . . Time!"

Clang went the gong, and the two desperate wizards stood face to face.

Madame Mim had gone on plotting during her rest. She had decided to try a new tack by leaving the offensive to Merlyn, beginning by assuming a defensive shape herself. She turned into a spreading oak.

Merlyn stood baffled under the oak for a few seconds. Then he most cheekily—and, as it turned out, rashly—became a powdery little blue-tit, which flew up and sat perkily on Madame Mim's branches. You could see the oak boiling with indignation for a moment; but then its rage became icy cold, and the poor little blue-tit was sitting not on an oak, but on a snake. The snake's mouth was open, and the bird was actually perching on its jaws. As the jaws clashed together, but only in the nick of time, the bird whizzed off as a gnat into the safe air. Madame Mim had got it on the run, however, and the speed of the contest now became bewildering. The quicker the attacker could assume a form, the less time the fugitive had to think of a form which would elude it, and now the changes were as quick as thought.

The gnat was scarcely in the air when the snake had turned into a toad whose curious tongue, rooted at the front instead of the back of the jaw, was already unrolling in the flick which would snap it in. The gnat, flustered by the sore pursuit, was bounced into an offensive role, and the hard-pressed Merlyn now stood before the toad in the shape of a mollern which could attack it. But Madame Mim was in her element. The game was going according to the normal rules now, and in less than an eye's blink the toad had turned into a peregrine falcon which was diving at two hundred and fifty miles an hour upon the heron's back. Poor Merlyn, beginning to lose his nerve, turned wildly into an elephant—this move usually won a little breathing space—but Madame Mim, relentless, changed from the falcon into an aullay on the instant. An aullay was as much bigger than an elephant as an elephant is larger than a sheep. It was a sort of horse with an elephant's trunk. Madame Mim raised this trunk in the air, gave a shriek like a railway engine, and rushed upon her panting foe. In a flick Merlyn had disappeared.

"One," said Hecate. "Two. Three. Four. Five. Six. Seven. Eight. Nine . . ."

But before the fatal Ten which would have counted him out, Merlyn reappeared in a bed of nettles, mopping his brow. He had been standing among them as a nettle.

The aullay saw no reason to change its shape. It rushed upon the man before it with another piercing scream. Merlyn vanished again just as the thrashing trunk descended, and all stood still a moment, looking about them, wondering where he would step out next.

"One," began Hecate again, but even as she proceeded with her counting, strange things began to happen. The aullay got hiccoughs, turned red, swelled visibly, began whooping, came out in spots, staggered three times, rolled its eyes, fell rumbling to the ground. It groaned, kicked, and said Farewell. The Wart cheered, Archimedes hooted till he cried, the gore-crow fell down dead, and Hecate, on the top of her ladder, clapped so much that she nearly tumbled off. It was a master stroke.

The ingenious magician had turned himself successively into the microbes, not yet discovered, of hiccoughs, scarlet fever, mumps, whooping cough, measles, and heat spots, and from a complication of all these complaints the infamous Madame Mim had immediately expired.

Blood Money

M. TIMOTHY O'KEEFE

Blood money.

That's what some small-minded people call it. I've never understood people like that. It's as good a way as any to earn money, and more painful than some.

I'm what's known as a PD or professional donor: I sell my blood to the highest bidder. Mine's a rare type, which only a few people in every thousand have. Some people consider me uncharitable for charging for it. Hah!

Oh, I donated once, during an emergency. Talk about a racket. The hospital called me in under some great humanitarian pretext, took my blood without paying me and then turned around and sold it to some poor guy mangled in an accident.

Most people think if they donate blood it's also given free to the person who needs it. Not so. Unless you've a friend that's specifically designated to receive your blood, the blood is sold.

So why give it away? I mean, everyone is entitled to a fair profit, but the hospitals are too much. The blood banks, however, are more honest. They at least pay you something and it doesn't cost a patient any more. A person is charged the same, whether the hospital got the blood free or purchased it.

The trouble is, blood banks don't pay much. They've got costs in handling and storing, so they pay only a part of what it's really worth. And since you're supposed to give blood only every six to eight weeks, it isn't any sort of way to get rich fast. It just brings in a little spending money.

That's why I was very interested to see the ad in this morning's newspaper. Some research outfit was willing to pay very high prices to donors who have special blood types. As much as $100 a week if you signed a contract to donate to them regularly.

So naturally I had to apply. I'd never seen anyone offer that much money before for blood. That was a deal I wanted in on.

I went down for them to run some preliminary tests. They said it looked promising but that I would need to come back at nine that evening so I could be tested further and interviewed by the Chief of Research. He was going to be too busy to see me before then.

So here I am, sitting in the waiting room of the blood bank waiting to see the guy. A hundred a week for almost nothing but staying alive—that's more than I could earn at some jobs.

"Doctor can see you now, Mr. Ashbury." At last. The nurse takes me down a winding hallway and into a small, well-lit room. She has me take off my coat and roll up my sleeves and then straps me to the table, which is something new.

"Why the straps?" I ask.

"So you won't run away," she laughs. And leaves, closing the door.

A real comic, that one. I hear a noise behind me and a fat cheerful-looking fellow is getting the needle ready to stick in my arm. He looks like he really enjoys his work. "Are you the Chief of Research?" I ask. "I'm supposed to deal only with him."

"Yes, Mr. Ashbury. I'm the man in charge. Now don't flinch—ah, wasn't that painless?"

I've got to admit he did it well, not like some guys who try over and over to pierce the vein like it was made of plastic. I always feel a little squeamish when the blood starts to flow through the tubes into the container, but I've found that if I watch it for a few seconds to reassure myself I'm not going to bleed to death I feel a lot better. It is kind of scary to see all that life pouring out of you.

The doctor seemed to be watching just as intently. Maybe too intently. "Excuse me, Doc, but do you feel okay? You seem to be sweating."

He wipes away a small trickle of saliva from his mouth and smiles an apology. "I haven't had breakfast yet. I was waiting for you, but evidently I'm hungrier than I thought. I'll just get a snack until you're ready."

With that he goes over to the small refrigerator

by his desk and takes out a small vial of red liquid and drinks it.

Suddenly I don't feel so well. That wasn't any grape juice he's just drunk. I've been in this business too long not to know the real stuff.

"Damn!" I say. "I think I want to leave." I reach for the strap across my chest but I can't unbuckle it with just one hand. He's at my side in an instant, pulling my hand away.

"That was unforgivable of me," he says. "I should have offered you a drink. How about a Bloody Mary?"

"You can't fool me," I shout. "That was whole blood you just drank. What kind of fiend are you?" I gulp. I think I know. Only one thing I've ever heard of has a breakfast like that this time of evening. "Maybe I will have that drink. How about a screwdriver."

"Excellent," he says. "I have some fresh orange juice just squeezed this afternoon." He smiles. "We like to have everything around here nice and fresh."

As he's fixing me a screwdriver I notice he's also putting a little vodka in another vial with red liquid for himself. If he's trying to fool me, it's too late. I *know*.

"Are you going to kill me?" I ask. "This may be more sanitary than biting me in the neck but it can drain me just as dry. And you can store what you don't need of me in the refrigerator until tomorrow—just like you did to that poor fellow!"

I look around the room closely for the first time. It's been soundproofed so no one can hear my screams. There aren't any windows. There's no way I can call for help. Then I remember what that nurse said when she strapped me in. They're all in on this!

He looks at me with some concern. "I can see you don't understand at all. Why would I want to kill you? That would only defeat my purpose in bringing you here."

He brings a chair over to sit next to me while we have our drinks. He raises the head of the table so I don't choke to death when I swallow, which seems a funny way of postponing the inevitable.

"I didn't mean for this to be such a shock to you. I had hoped to break it to you gradually. I was simply hungrier than I realized."

"But that makes you a vampire! Or a ghoul or something!"

"A vampire, yes. But please don't confuse me with some of that other despicable trash. They have absolutely no class. Imagine eating a corpse! It's enough to make you ill. A revolting, barbaric habit."

Somehow I think I'm hearing things. His way's any better? "I won't let you keep me trapped here to raise me like a fat pig to be butchered off slowly. I'll kill myself first," I tell him bravely.

He shakes his head sadly. "Not you too. I can see you've been seeing too many old horror movies. Bram Stoker did a great disservice to my race when he wrote that stupid *Dracula*. It's filled with so many inaccuracies about our habits I'm not surprised you're upset. He makes me so mad I could turn him over in his grave."

"Your fangs—where are your fangs? I know how you finish off your victims!"

"That old legend, still. We haven't had fangs for centuries. I was once just as human as you are, Mr. Ashbury. Can you imagine yourself continually wearing a set of fangs? You'd cut your lips to shreds. And you would have to sleep with your mouth open, which would be entirely too dangerous. The snoring might attract attention to your hiding place while you slept through the day."

He walks over to his desk, opens the drawer and pulls out a set of what look like fangs. "Through the normal evolutionary pattern we have lost the need for fangs as we've become more specialized in the way we secure blood. These, however, are still kept for emergencies. You can never tell when you might be in a pinch sometime and you need to put the bite on somebody," he chuckles.

He slips the false fangs into his mouth. I have to admit they look uncomfortable. If you were out of practice they could hurt you severely.

"But you have to sleep during the day," I say. "That part's right. That's why you couldn't see me until tonight. If you get caught in the sun you'll crumble into dust!" I say smugly.

"Yes, though I don't know why you humans take such pride in being able to endure the sun. It dries *your* skin rather badly and causes it to age prematurely. It just works faster on us."

By now I'm really intrigued with what he's telling me. I even get a little carried away. "Change yourself into a bat. I want to see that!"

He shakes his head sadly. "It's been so long since I tried that I'm not sure I could anymore. It's too dangerous these days. It's too easy to impale yourself on a television antenna. Plus the quality of the air up there is awful. Not like the old days when it was a real joy to go for a spin.

"It's gotten so bad," he continues, "that if I wanted to go to the beach people would start shooting at me because they would think I might carry rabies. Being a vampire isn't as much fun as it used to be."

For some reason I feel a little sorry for him. I mean, somehow it isn't fair. He can't help what he is. "Then why do you keep at it? If it's got so bad, why not give up?"

He took another sip of his drink before answering. "I've thought about it sometimes. But I've been at this for so long I've grown used to it. And let's face it, after you've been a vampire, what's left? Once that's over, you're really finished."

I nodded slowly. There was a lot of truth to that. "Why do you want me? How am I supposed to be a part of all this?"

He came over to check my needle before answering. "Just a bit more and that will be all for this time," he said reassuringly. "Don't worry, Mr. Ashbury. What I have to offer you is a straight business proposition. Vampires have had to become modern with the times. No more skulking around parks and preying on young women. Too much bad publicity. Besides, would you care to walk alone through some of our city parks? They're just not safe anymore.

"I now have an opening and I need a new man

like you. I could use some new blood, you might say," he chuckles. "One of my donors recently passed away—I assure you I had nothing to do with it—and I need a replacement." He stops suddenly. "Do you realize how much blood a vampire needs to keep himself going, Mr. Ashbury?"

I tell him I haven't thought about it much.

"We need at least two pints of fresh whole blood every day. That's quite a lot. Furthermore, I can drink only a special quality of blood due to some sort of deficiency in my metabolism. It's like some of you humans can't eat sugar because it might prove fatal. In the same way, I can only drink certain types of blood. You might be interested to know that only a half of a percent of the population has your kind of blood."

Finally I think I see what he's driving at. He smiles at my understanding. "Now I think you're beginning to comprehend. It would be foolish for me to drain anyone completely. It would only dry up my supply. Eventually there would be no one left and I too would die. So you see, it is just as much in my interest to keep you living as it is yours to remain that way. I *need* you alive, Mr. Ashbury. And I need you wanting to give me some of your blood every eight weeks."

He walks around to stand directly over me. "What I'm doing is simple. I have contracted with a sizable group of people to come here periodically to give a pint of blood. In return I pay you $100 a week as long as you continue to donate. There are no strings. There is one thing I must insist on, and that is that you be honest with me. If anyone else offers you more to start supplying them, come to me and I will raise the price."

"You mean there are more of you who work like this?"

"Of course, Mr. Ashbury. This blood bank is just a front. Who do you think supplies others of my kind? Why do you think no one has heard of vampires for years? We've become modern."

It makes sense. I say, "You have to earn a living some way to be able to pay your blood bill. It must be rather expensive."

"It is. And there aren't too many options on the kind of employment we 'night people' have. They all pay far too little for what I require. Would you believe that I was once a night watchman in a hospital? I had to give it up when they caught me drinking on the job. There was just so much available I couldn't resist a taste." He sighed. "It was like working in a candy factory. It was too much of a good thing to keep from sampling the product."

"Well, if this is how you stay alive, how do your friends make enough money to keep body and soul together?" I winced when I realized what I'd just said. Vampires don't have souls.

He took another drink, paused a moment before answering. "I guess it's safe to tell you if you're going to be one of us. You are, aren't you?"

"For a hundred a week? Are you kidding? Of course."

"Very well. You've heard of cat burglars before, haven't you? Well, my friends are 'bat burglars.'

Instead of sneaking through windows and across dangerous ledges they simply fly down chimneys and steal a few jewels. Then they bring them to me and I fence them. It's kind of a bartering situation, really. Everyone ends up getting what he wants, including you, Mr. Ashbury."

"But what about the ones whose jewels are stolen? It doesn't do them much good."

"The insurance, of course. Most of them file a claim for more than their stuff is worth. They don't suffer. It keeps up the demand for insurance, too, since everyone is afraid they might be the next victim. That's how the insurance companies keep getting so many new clients. You could almost say we're good for business."

I shake my head. "The way you explain it, the whole thing seems almost necessary for the economy." I glance at the tube draining the liquid from my arm. "Don't you think that's enough?"

"Yes, certainly. I wasn't paying attention." He pulls the needle from my arm and pours the liquid into another container.

"Now, Mr. Ashbury, here's your money. It's in cash, you'll notice. It's up to you whether you report it to the tax people."

Now, that's all right. "A toast!" I suggest. "To a lasting partnership," I say and drain my glass.

"To a long life, Mr. Ashbury. For both of us."

Suddenly I don't feel so good. That's me he's just drunk.

His Coat So Gay

STERLING LANIER

After many years in Her Majesty's service, the fictional Englishman Brigadier Donald Ffellowes is now retired and living in New York City. At his club he is in the habit of thrilling his fellow members with tales of macabre adventures in his career, all supposedly true. The story that follows, addressed to a group of American club members, is one of these.

In the early days of your, and indeed everyone's, Great Depression, I was the most junior military attache of our Washington embassy. It was an agreeable part of my duties to mix socially as much as I could with Americans of my own age. One way of doing this was hunting, fox-hunting to be more explicit. I used to go out with the Middleburg Hunt and while enjoying the exercise, I made a number of friends as well.

One of them was a man whom I shall call Canler

Waldron. That's not even an anagram, but sounds vaguely like his real name. He was my own age and very good company. He was supposed to be putting in time as a junior member of your State Department.

It was immediately obvious that he was extremely well off. Most people, of course, had been at least affected a trifle by the Crash, if not a whole lot, but it was plain that whatever Can's financial basis was, it had hardly been shaken. Small comments were revealing, especially his puzzlement when, as often happened, others pleaded lack of funds to explain some inability to do a trip or to purchase something. He was, I may add, the most generous of men financially, and without being what you'd call a "sucker," he was very easy to leave with the check, so much so one had to guard against it.

He was pleasant-looking: black-haired, narrow-faced, dark brown eyes, a generalized North European type and as I said about my own age, barely twenty-six. And what a magnificent rider! I'm not bad, or wasn't then, but I've never seen anyone to match Canler Waldron. No fence ever bothered him and he always led the field, riding so easily that he hardly appeared to be conscious of what he was doing. It got so that he became embarrassed by the attention and used to pull his horse in order to stay back. Of course he was magnificently mounted; he had a whole string of big black hunters, his own private breed, he said. But there were others out who had fine "cattle" too; no, he was simply a superb rider.

We were chatting one fall morning after a very dull run and I asked him why he always wore a black hunting coat of a non-hunt member. I knew he belonged to some hunt or other and didn't understand why he never used their colors.

"Highly embarrassing to explain to you, Donald, of all people," he said, but he was smiling. "My family were Irish and very patriotic during our Revolution. No pink coats ("pink" being the term for hunting red) for us. Too close to the hated Redcoat Army in looks, see? So we wear light green and I frankly get damned tired of being asked what it is. That's all."

I was amused for several reasons and said, "Of course I understand. Some of our own hunts wear other colors, you know. But I thought green coats were for foot hounds, beagles, bassets and such?"

"Ours is much lighter, like grass, with buff lapels," he said. He seemed a little ill at ease for some reason, as our horses shifted and stamped under the hot Virginia sun. "It's a family hunt, you see. No non-Waldron can wear the coat. This sounds pretty snobby, so again, I avoid questions by not wearing it except at home. Betty feels the same way and she hates black. Here she comes now. What did you think of the ride, Sis?"

"Not very exciting," she said quietly, looking around so that she should not be convicted of rudeness to our hosts. I haven't mentioned Betty Waldron, have I? Even after all these years, it's still painful.

She was nineteen years old, very pale, and no sun ever raised so much as a freckle. Her eyes were almost black, her hair midnight and her voice very gentle and sad. She was quiet, seldom smiled and when she did my heart turned over. Usually, her thoughts were miles away and she seemed to walk in a dream. She also rode superbly, almost absent-mindedly, to look at her.

I was a poor devil of an artillery subaltern, few prospects save for my pay, but I could dream, as long as I kept my mouth shut. She seemed to like me as much, or even more, than the gaudy lads who were always flocking about, and I felt I had a tiny, the smallest grain of hope. I'd never said a thing. I knew already the family must be staggeringly rich and I had my pride. But also, as I say, my dreams.

"Let's ask Donald home and give him some real sport," I suddenly heard Can say to her.

"When?" she asked sharply, looking hard at him.

"How about the end of cubbing season? Last week in October. Get the best of both sports, adult and young. Hounds will be in good condition and it's our best time of year." He smiled at me and patted his horse. "What say, Limey? Like some real hunting, eight hours sometimes?"

I was delighted and surprised, because I'd heard several people fishing rather obviously for invitations to the Waldron place at one time or another and all being politely choked off. I had made up my mind never to place myself where such a rebuff could strike me. There was a goodish number of fortune-hunting Europeans about just then, some of them English, and they made me a trifle ill. But I was surprised and hurt too, by Betty's reaction.

"Not this fall, Can," she said, her face even whiter than usual. "Not–this–fall!" The words were stressed separately and came out with an intensity I can't convey.

"As the head of the family, I'm afraid what I say goes," said Canler in a voice I'd certainly never heard him use before. It was heavy and dominating, even domineering. As I watched, quite baffled, she choked back a sob and urged her horse away from us. In a moment her slender black back and shining topper were lost in the milling sea of the main body of the hunt. I was really hurt badly.

"Now look here, old boy," I said. "I don't know what's going on, but I can't possibly accept your invitation under these circumstances. Betty obviously loathes the idea and I wouldn't dream of coming against her slightest wish."

He urged his horse over until we were only a yard apart. "You must, Donald. You don't understand. I don't like letting out family secrets, but I'm going to have to in this case. Betty was very roughly treated by a man last year, in the fall. A guy who seemed to like her and then just walked out, without a word, and disappeared. I know you'll never speak of this to her and she'd rather die than say anything to you. But I haven't been able to get her interested in things ever since. You're the first man she's liked from that time to this and you've got to help me pull her out of this depression. Surely you've noticed how vague and dreamy she is? She's living in a world of unreality, trying to shut out unhappiness. I can't get her to see a doctor and even if I could, it probably wouldn't do any good. What she needs is some decent man being kind to her in the same surroundings she was made unhappy in. Can you see why I need you as a friend so badly?" He was damned earnest and it was impossible not to be touched.

"Well, that's all very well," I mumbled, "but she's still dead set against my coming, you know. I simply can't come in the face of such opposition. You mentioned yourself as head of the family. Do I take it that your parents are dead? Because if so, then Betty is my hostess. It won't do, damn it all."

"Now look," he said. "Don't turn me down. By tomorrow morning she'll ask you herself, I swear. I promise that if she doesn't the whole thing's off. Will you come if she does and give me a hand at cheering her up? And we are orphans, by the way, just us two."

Of course I agreed. I was wild to come. To get leave would be easy. There was nothing much but routine at the embassy anyway and mixing with people like the Waldrons was as much a part of my duties as going to any Fort Leavenworth maneuvers.

And sure enough, Betty rang me up at my Washington flat the next morning and apologized for her behavior the previous day. She sounded very dim and tired but perfectly all right. I asked her twice if she was sure she wanted my company and she repeated that she did, still apologizing for the day before. She said she had felt feverish and didn't know why she'd spoken as she had. This was good enough for me and so it was settled.

Thus, in the last week in October, I found myself hunting the coverts of—well, call it the valley of Waldrondale. What a glorious, mad time it was! The late Indian summer lingered and each cold night gave way to a lovely misty dawn. The main Waldron lands lay in the hollow of a spur of the Appalachian range. Apparently some early Waldron, an emigrant from Ireland during the 1600's, I gathered, had gone straight west into Indian territory and somehow laid claim to a perfectly immense tract of country. What is really odd is that the red men seemed to feel it was all fine, that he should do so.

"We always got along with our Indians," Canler told me once. "Look around the valley at the faces, my own included. There's some Indian blood in all of us. A branch of the lost Erie nation, before the Iroquois destroyed them, according to the family records."

It was quite true that when one looked, the whole valley indeed appeared to have a family resemblance. The women were very pale and both sexes were black-haired and dark-eyed, with lean, aquiline features. Many of them, apparently local farmers, rode with the hunt, and fine riders they were too—well-mounted and fully familiar with field etiquette.

Waldrondale was a great, heart-shaped valley, of perhaps eight thousand acres. The Waldrons leased some of it to cousins and farmed some themselves. They owned still more land outside the actual valley, but that was all leased. It was easy to see that in Waldrondale itself they were actually rulers. Although both Betty and Can were called by their first names, every one of the valley dwellers was ready and willing to drop whatever he or she was doing at a moment's notice to oblige either of them in the smallest way. It was not subservience exactly, but instead almost an eagerness, of the sort a monarch might have gotten in the days when kings were sacred beings. Canler shrugged when I mentioned how the matter struck me.

"We've just been here a long time, that's all. They've simply got used to us telling them what to do. When the first Waldron came over from Galway, a lot of retainers seem to have come with him. So it's not really a strictly normal American situation." He looked lazily at me. "Hope you don't think we're too effete and baronial here, now that England's becoming so democratized?"

"Not at all," I said quickly and the subject was changed. There had been an unpleasant undertone in his speech—almost jeering—and for some reason he seemed rather irritated.

What wonderful hunting we had! The actual members of the hunt, those who wore the light green jackets, were only a dozen or so, mostly close relatives of Canler's and Betty's. When we had started the first morning at dawn I'd surprised them all, for I was then a full member of the Duke of Beaufort's pack, and as a joke more than anything else had brought the blue and yellow-lapelled hunting coat along. The joke was that I had been planning to show them, the Waldrons, one of our own variant colors all along, ever since I had heard about theirs.

They were all amazed at seeing me not only not in black, but in "non-red" so to speak. The little withered huntsman, a local farmer named McColl, was absolutely taken aback and for some reason seemed frightened. He made a curious remark, of which I caught only two words, "Sam Haines," and then made a sign which I had no trouble at all interpreting. Two fingers at either end of a fist have always been an attempt to ward off the evil eye, or some other malign spiritual influence. I said nothing at the time, but during dinner asked Betty who Sam Haines was and what had made old McColl so nervous about my blue coat. Betty's reaction was ever more peculiar. She muttered something about a local holiday and also that my coat was the "wrong color for an Englishman," and then abruptly changed the subject. Puzzled, I looked up, to notice that all conversation seemed to have died at the rest of the big table. There were perhaps twenty guests, all the regular hunt members and some more besides from the outlying parts of the valley. I was struck by the intensity of the very similar faces, male and female, all staring at us, lean, pale and dark-eyed, all with that coarse raven hair. For a moment I had a most peculiar feeling that I had blundered into a den of some dangerous creatures or other, not unlike a wolf. Then Canler laughed from the head of the table and conversation started again. The illusion was broken, as a thrown pebble shatters a mirrored pool of water, and I promptly forgot it.

The golden, wonderful days passed as October drew to a close. We were always up before dawn

and hunted the great vale of Waldrondale sometimes until noon. Large patches of dense wood had
been left deliberately uncleared here and there and
made superb coverts. I never had such a good going,
not even in Leicestershire at its best. And I was with
Betty, who seemed happy, too. But although we
drew almost the entire valley at one time or another
there was one area we avoided, and it puzzled me
to the point of asking Can about it one morning.

Directly behind the Big House (it had no other
name) the ground rose very sharply in the direction
of the high blue hills beyond. But a giant hedge,
all tangled and overgrown, barred access to whatever lay up the slope. The higher hills angled down,
as it were, as if to enclose the house and grounds,
two arms of high rocky ground almost reaching the
level of the house on either side. Yet it was evident
that an area of some considerable extent, a smallish
plateau in fact, lay directly behind the house, between it and the sheer slopes of the mountain, itself
some jagged outlier of the great Appalachian chain.
And the huge hedge could only have existed for
the purpose of barring access to this particular piece
of land.

"It's a sanctuary," Canler said when I asked him.
"The family has a burial plot there and we always
go there on—on certain days. It's been there since
we settled the area, has some first-growth timber
among other things, and we like to keep it as it is.
But I'll show it to you before you leave if you're
really interested." His voice was incurious and flat,
but again I had the feeling, almost a sixth sense if

you like, that I had somehow managed to both annoy and, odder, amuse him. I changed the subject and we spoke of the coming day's sport.

One more peculiar thing occurred on that day in the late afternoon. Betty and I had got a bit separated from the rest of the hunt, a thing I didn't mind one bit, and we also were some distance out from the narrow mouth of the valley proper, for the fox had run very far indeed. As we rode toward home under the warm sun, I noticed that we were passing a small, white, country church, wooden, you know, and rather shabby. As I looked, the minister, parson, or what have you, appeared on the porch, and seeing us, stood still, staring. We were not more than thirty feet apart, for the dusty path, hardly a road at all, ran right next to the church. The minister was a tired-looking soul of about fifty, dressed in an ordinary suit but with a Roman collar, just like the C. of E. curate at home.

But the man's expression! He never looked at me, but he stared at Betty, never moving or speaking, and the venom in his eyes was unmistakable. Hatred and contempt mingled with loathing.

Our horses had stopped and in the silence they fidgeted and stamped. I looked at Betty and saw a look of pain on her face, but she never spoke or moved either. I decided to break the silence myself.

"Good day, Padre," I said breezily. "Nice little church you have here. A jolly spot, lovely trees and all." I expect I sounded half-witted.

He turned his gaze on me and it changed utterly. The hatred vanished and instead I saw the face of a decent, kindly man, yes and a deeply troubled one. He raised one hand and I thought for a startled moment he actually was going to bless me, don't you know, but he evidently thought better of it. Instead he spoke, plainly addressing me alone.

"For the next forty-eight hours this church will remain open. And I will be here."

With that, he turned on his heel and re-entered the church, shutting the door firmly behind him.

"Peculiar chap, that," I said to Betty. "Seems to have a bit of a down on you, too, if his nasty look was any indication. Is he out of his head, or what? Perhaps I ought to speak to Can, eh?"

"No," she said quickly, putting her hand on my arm. "You mustn't; promise me you won't say anything to him about this, not a word!"

"Of course I won't, Betty, but what on earth is wrong with the man? All that mumbo-jumbo about his confounded church bein' open?"

"He—well, he doesn't like any of our family, Donald. Perhaps he has reason. Lots of the people outside the valley aren't too fond of the Waldrons. And the Depression hasn't helped matters. Can won't cut down on high living and of course hungry people who see us are furious. Don't let's talk any more about it. Mr. Andrews is a very decent man and I don't want Canler to hear about this. He might be angry and do something unpleasant. No more talk now. Come on, the horses are rested. I'll race you to the main road."

The horses were *not* rested and we both knew it,

but I would never refuse her anything. By the time we rejoined the main body of the hunt, the poor beasts were blown, and we suffered a lot of chaff, mostly directed at me, for not treating our mounts decently.

The next day was the thirty-first of October. My stay had only two more days to run and I could hardly bear to think of leaving. But I felt glorious too. The previous night, as I had thrown the bed-clothes back, preparatory to climbing in, a small packet had been revealed. Opening it, I had found a worn, tiny cross on a chain, both silver and ob-viously very old. I recognized the cross as being of the ancient Irish or Gaelic design, rounded and with a circle in the center where the arms joined. There was a note in a delicate hand I knew well, since I'd saved every scrap of paper I'd ever received from her.

"Wear this for me always and say nothing to anyone."

Can you imagine how marvelous life seemed? The next hunt morning was so fine it could hardly have been exceeded. But even if it had been terrible and I'd broken a leg, I don't think I'd have noticed. I was wearing Betty's family token, sent to *me*, se-cretly under my shirt, and I came very close to singing aloud. She said nothing to me, save for pol-ite banalities, and looked tired, as if she'd not slept too well.

As we rode past a lovely field of gathered shocks of maize, your "corn," you know, I noticed all the jolly pumpkins still left lying about in the fields and asked my nearest neighbor, one of the younger cousins, if the local kids didn't use them for Halloween as I'd been told in the papers.

"Today?" he said, and then gobbled the same words used by the old huntsman, "Sam Haines," or perhaps "Hayne."

"We don't call it that," he added stiffly and before I could ask why or anything else, spurred his horse and rode ahead. I was beginning to wonder, in a vague sort of way, if all this isolation really could be good for people. Canler and Betty seemed increasingly moody and indeed the whole crowd appeared subject to odd moods.

Perhaps a bit inbred, I thought. *I must try and get Betty out of here.* Now apparently I'd offended someone by mentioning Hallowe'en, which, it occurred to me in passing, was that very evening. "Sam Haines" indeed!

Well, I promptly forgot all that when we found, located a fox, you know, and the chase started. It was a splendid one and long and we had a very late lunch. I got a good afternoon rest, since Canler had told me we were having a banquet that evening. "A farewell party for you, Donald," he said, "and a special one. We don't dress up much, but tonight we'll have a sort of hunt ball, eh?"

I'd seen no preparations for music, but the Big House was so really big that the London Symphony could have been hid somewhere about.

I heard the dinner gong as I finished dressing and when I came down to the main living room, all were assembled, the full hunt, with all the men in their soft emerald green dress coats, to which my blue made a mild contrast. To my surprise, a number of children, although not small ones, were there also, all in party dress, eyes gleaming with excitement. Betty looked lovely in an emerald evening dress, but also very wrought up and her eyes did not meet mine. Once again, a tremendous desire to protect her and get her out of this interesting but rather curious clan came over me.

But Can was pushing his way through the throng and he took me by the elbow. "Come and be toasted, Donald, as the only outsider," he said, smiling. "Here's the family punch and the family punchbowl too, something few others have ever seen."

At a long table in a side alcove stood an extraordinary bowl, a huge stone thing, with things like runes scratched around the rim. Behind it, in his "greens" but bareheaded, stood the little withered huntsman, McColl. It was he who filled a squat goblet, but as he did so and handed it to me, his eyes narrowed and he hissed something inaudible over the noise behind me. It sounded like "watch." I was alerted and when he handed me the curious stone cup I knew why. There was a folded slip of paper under the cup's base, which I took as I accepted the cup itself. Can, who stood just behind me, could have seen nothing.

I'm rather good at conjuring tricks and it was only a moment before I was able to pass my hand over my forehead and read the note at the same instant. The message was simple, the reverse of Alice's on the bottle.

"Drink nothing." That was all, but it was enough to send a thrill through my veins. I was sure of two things. McColl had never acted this way on his own hook. Betty, to whom the man was obviously devoted, was behind this.

I was in danger. I knew it. All the vague uneasiness I had suppressed during my stay, the peculiar stares, the cryptic remarks, the attitude of the local minister we had seen, all coalesced into something ominous, inchoate but menacing. These cold, good-looking people were not my friends, if indeed they were anyone's. I looked casually about while pretending to sip from my cup. Between me and each one of the three exits, a group of men were standing, chatting and laughing, accepting drinks from trays passed by servants, but *never moving*. As my brain began to race overtime, I actually forgot my warning and sipped from my drink. It was like nothing I have had before or since, being pungent, sweet and at the same time almost perfumed, but not in an unpleasant way. I managed to avoid swallowing all but a tiny bit, but even that was wildly exhilarating, making my face flush and the blood roar through my veins. It must have showed, I expect, for I saw my host half smile and others too, as they raised their cups to me. The sudden wave of anger I felt did not show, but now I really commenced to think.

I turned and presented my almost full goblet to McColl again as if asking for more. Without batting an eye, he *emptied* it behind the cover of the great bowl, as if cleaning out some dregs, and refilled it.

The little chap had brains. As again I raised the cup to my lips, I saw the smile appear on Can's face once more. My back was to McColl, blocking him off from the rest of the room, and this time his rasping, penetrating whisper was easy to hear.

"After dinner, be paralyzed, stiff, frozen in your seat. You can't move, understand?"

I made a circle with my fingers behind my back to show I understood, and then walked out into the room to meet Canler, who was coming toward me.

"Don't stand at the punch all evening, Donald," he said, laughing. "You have a long night ahead, you know." But now his laughter was mocking and his lean, handsome face was suddenly a mask of cruelty and malign purpose. As we moved about together, the faces and manners of the others, both men and women, even the children and servants, were the same, and I wondered that I had ever thought any of them friendly. Under their laughter and banter, I felt contempt, yes and hatred and triumph too, mixed with a streak of pure nastiness. I was the stalled ox, flattered, fattened and fed, and the butchers were amused. They knew my fate, but I would not know until the door of the abattoir closed behind me. But the ox was not quite helpless yet, nor was the door quite slammed shut. I noticed Betty had gone and when I made some comment or other, Can laughed and told me she was checking dinner preparations, as indeed any hostess might. I played my part as well as I could, and apparently well enough. McColl gave me bogus refills when we were alone and I tried to seem excited, full of *joie de vivre,* you know. Whatever other effect was expected was seemingly reserved for after dinner.

Eventually, about nine I should think, we went in to dinner; myself carefully shepherded between several male cousins. These folk were not leaving much to chance, whatever their purpose.

The great dining room was a blaze of candles and gleaming silver and crystal. I was seated next to Betty at one end of the long table and Canler took the other. Servants began to pour wine and the dinner commenced. At first, the conversation and laughter were, to outward appearances, quite normal. The shrill laughter of the young rose above the deeper tones of their elders. Indeed the sly, feral glances of the children as they watched me surreptitiously were not the least of my unpleasant impressions. Once again and far more strongly, the feeling of being in a den of some savage and predatory brutes returned to me, and this time, it did not leave.

At my side, Betty was the exception. Her face never looked lovelier—ivory white in the candle glow, and calm, as if whatever had troubled her earlier had gone. She did not speak much, but her eyes met mine frankly, and I felt stronger, knowing that in the woman I loved, whatever came, I had at least one ally.

I have said that as the meal progressed, so too did the quiet. I had eaten a fairish amount, but barely tasted any of the wines from the battery of glasses at my place. As dessert was cleared off, amid almost total silence, I became aware that I had better start playing my other role, for every eye was now trained at my end of the table.

Turning to the girl, an unmarried cousin, on my right side, I spoke slowly and carefully, as one intoxicated.

"My goodness, that punch must have been strong! I can scarcely move my hand, d'you know. Good thing we don't have to ride tonight, eh?"

Whatever possessed me to say *that,* I can't think, but my partner stared at me and then broke into a peal of cold laughter. As she did so, choking with her own amusement, the man on her far side, who had heard me also, repeated it to his neighbors. In an instant the whole table was aripple with sinister delight, and I could see Can at the far end, his white teeth gleaming as he caught the joke. I revolved my head slowly and solemnly in apparent puzzlement, and the laughter grew. I could see two of the waiters laughing in a far corner. And then it ceased.

A great bell or chime tolled somewhere, not too far off, and there was complete silence, as if by magic. Suddenly I was aware of Canler, who had risen at his place and had raised his hands, as if in an invocation.

"The hour returns," he cried. "The Blessed Feast is upon us, the Feast of Sam'hain. My people, hence to your duties, to your robes, to the sacred park of the *Sheade!* Go, for the hour comes and passes!"

It was an effort to sit still while this rigamarole went on, but I remembered the earlier warnings and froze in my seat, blinking stupidly. It was as well, for four of the men-servants, all large, now stood behind and beside my chair. In an instant the room was empty, save for these four, myself and my host, who now strode the length of the table to stare down at me, his eyes filled with anger and contempt. Before I could even move, he had struck me over the face with his open hand.

"You, you English boor, would raise your eyes to the last princess of the Firbolgs, whose stock used yours as the meat and beasts of burden they are before Rome was even a village! Last year we had another one like you, and his polo-playing friends at Hicksville are still wondering where he went!" He laughed savagely and struck me again. I can tell you chaps, I learned real self-control in that moment! I never moved, but gazed up at him, my eyes blank, registering vacuous idiocy.

"The mead of the *Dagda* keeps its power," he said. "Bring him along, you four, the Great Hour passes!"

Keeping limp, I allowed myself to be lifted and carried from the room. Through the great dark house, following that false friend, its master, we went, until at last we climbed a broad stair and emerged under the frosty October stars. Before us lay the towering, overgrown hedge, and now I learned the secret of it. A great gate, overgrown with vines so as to be invisible when shut, had been opened and before me lay the hidden place of the House of Waldron. This is what I saw:

An avenue of giant oaks marched a quarter mile to a circular space where towered black tumuli of stone rose against the night sky. As I was borne toward these monoliths, the light of great fires was kindled on either side as I passed, and from them came an acrid, evil reek which caught at the throat. Around and over them leapt my fellow dinner guests and the servants wearing scanty green tunics, young and old together, their voices rising in a wild screaming chant, unintelligible, but regular and rhythmic. Canler had vanished momentarily, but now I heard his voice ahead of us. He must have been gone longer than I thought, for when those carrying me reached the circle of standing stones, he was standing outlined against the largest fire of all, which blazed, newly kindled, behind him. I saw the cause of the horrid stench, for instead of logs, were burning white dry bones, a great mountain of them. Next to him stood Betty and both of them had their arms raised and were singing the same wild chant as the crowd behind me.

I was slammed to the ground by my guards but held erect and immovable so that I had a good chance to examine the two heirs of one of the finest families in the modern United States.

Both were barefoot and wore thigh-length green tunics, his apparently wool, but hers silk or something like it, with her ivory body gleaming through it almost as if she were nude. Upon her breast and belly were marks of gold, like some strange, uncouth writing, clearly visible through the gauzy fabric. Her black hair was unbound and poured in waves over her shoulders. Canler wore upon his neck a massive circular torque, also of gold, and on his head a coronal wreath, apparently of autumn leaves. In Betty's right hand was held a golden sceptre, looking like a crude attempt to form a giant stalk of wheat. She waved this in rhythm as they sang.

Behind me the harsh chorus rose in volume and I knew the rest of the pack, for that's how I thought of them, were closing in. The noise rose to a crescendo, then ceased. Only the crackling of the great, reeking fire before me broke the night's silence. Then Canler raised his hands again in invocation and began a solitary chant in the strange harsh tongue they had used before. It was brief and when it came to an end, he spoke again, but in English this time.

"I call to Sam'hain, Lord of the Dead, I Tuathal, the Seventieth and One Hundred, of the line of Miled, of the race of Goedel Glas, last true *Ardr'i* of ancient Erin, Supreme Vate of the *Corcou Firbolgi*. Oh, Lord from Beyond, who has preserved my ancient people and nourished them in plenty, the bone-fires greet the night, your sacrifice awaits you!" He fell silent and Betty stepped forward. In her left hand she now held a small golden sickle, and very gently she pricked my forehead three times, in three places. Then she stepped back and called out in her clear voice.

"I, Morrigu, Priestess and Bride of the Dead, have prepared the sacrifice. Let the Horses of the Night attend!"

D'ye know, all I could think of was some homework I'd done on your American Constitution, in which Washington advocated separation of church and state? The human mind is a wonderful thing! Quite apart from the reek of the burning bones, though, I knew a stench of a spiritual sort. I was seeing something old here, old beyond knowledge, old and evil. I felt that somehow not only my body was in danger.

Now I heard the stamp of hooves. From one side, snorting and rearing, a great black horse was led into the firelight by a half-naked boy, who had trouble with the beast, but still held him. The horse was saddled and bridled and I knew him at once. It was Bran, the hunter I'd been lent all week. Behind him, I could hear other horses moving.

"Mount him," shouted Canler, or Tuathal, as he now called himself. With that, I was lifted into the saddle, where I swayed, looking as doped and helpless as I could. Before I could move, my hands were caught and lashed together at the wrists with leather cords, then in turn tied loosely to the headstall, giving them a play of some inches but no more. The reins were looped up and knotted. Then my host stepped up to my knee and glared up at me.

"The Wild Hunt rides, Slave and Outlander! You are the quarry, and two choices lie before you, both being death. For if we find you, death by these . . ." And he waved a curious spear, short and broad in the blade.

"But *others* hunt on this night, and maybe when Those Who Hunt Without Riders come upon your track, you will wish for these points instead. Save for children's toys, the outside world has long forgotten their Christian Feast of All Hallows. How long then have they forgot that which inspired it, ten thousand and more years before the Nazarene was slain? Now—ride and show good sport to the Wild Hunt!"

With that someone gave Bran a frightful cut over the croup, and he bounded off into the dark, almost unseating me in the process. I had no idea where we were going, except that it was not back down the avenue of trees and the blazing fires. But I soon saw that at least two riders were herding me away at an angle down the hill, cutting at Bran's flanks with whips when he veered from the course they had set. Twice the whips caught my legs, but the boots saved me from the worst of it.

Eventually, we burst out into a glade near the southern spur of the mountain and I saw another, smaller gate had been opened in the great hedge. Through this my poor brute was flogged, but once through it I was alone. The Big House was invisible around a curve of the hill, and no lights marked its presence.

"Ride hard, Englishman," called one of my herdsmen. "Two deaths follow on your track." With that, they turned back and I heard the gate slam. At the same time, I heard something else. Far off in the night I heard the shrill whinnying of a horse. Mingled with it and nearer was the sound of a horn, golden and clear. The horse cry was like that of no horse I have ever heard, a savage screaming noise which cut into my eardrums and raised the hackles even further on my back. At the same time I made a new discovery.

Some sharp thing had been poking into my left thigh ever since I was placed on the horse. Even in the starlight I now could see the reason. The haft of a heavy knife projected under my leg, apparently taped to the saddle! By stretching and bending my body, I could just free it and once free I cut the lead which tethered my wrists to the headstall. As I did so, I urged Bran with my knees downhill and to the right, keeping close to the trees which grew unclipped at the base of the mountain spur. I knew there was little time to waste, for the sound of galloping horses was coming through the night, far off, but drawing nearer by the instant! It might be the twentieth century outside the valley, but I knew it would be the last of me if that pack of green-clad maniacs ever caught up with me. The Wild Hunt was not a joke at this point!

As I saw it I had three secret assets. One, the knife, a sturdy piece of work with an eight-inch blade, which I now held in my teeth and tried to use to saw my wrists apart. The other was the fact that I have a good eye for ground and I had ridden the length and breadth of the valley for a week. While not as familiar with the area as those who now hunted me over it like a rabbit, I was, nevertheless, not a stranger and I fancied I could find my way even at night. My third ace was Betty. What she could do, I had no idea, but I felt sure she would do something.

The damned leather cords simply could not be cut while Bran moved, even at a walk, and I was forced to stop. It only took a second's sawing, for the knife was sharp, and I was free. I was in deep shadows, and I listened intently, while I unknotted the reins.

The sound of many horses galloping was still audible through the quiet night but it was no nearer, indeed the reverse. It now came from off to my left and somewhat lower down the valley. I was baffled by this, but only for a moment. Canler and his jolly group wanted a good hunt. Drugged as I was supposed to be, it would never do to follow directly on my track. Instead, they were heading to cut me off from the mouth of the valley, after which they could return at leisure and hunt me down. All of this and much more passed through my mind in seconds, you know.

My next thought was the hills, In most places, the encircling wall of mountain was far too steep for a horse. But I could leave Bran behind and most of the ground ought to be possible for an active chap on foot. By dawn I could be well out of reach of this murderous gang. As the thought crossed my mind, I urged Bran toward the nearest wall of rock. We crossed a little glade and approached the black mass of the slope, shrouded in more trees at the base, and I kept my eye peeled for trouble. But it was my mount who found it.

He suddenly snorted and checked, stamping his feet, refusing to go a foot forward. I drew the knife from my belt, also alerted—and by a sudden awakening of a sense far older than anything merely physical. Ahead of us lay a menace of a different sort than the hunters of Waldrondale. I remembered my quondam host threatening me that something else was hunting that night, and also that the men who had driven me through the hedge called after me that *two* deaths were on my track.

Before me, as I sat, frozen in the saddle, something moved in the shadows. It was large, but its exact shape was not easy to make out. I was conscious of a sudden feeling of intense cold, something I've experienced once or twice. I now know this to mean that one of what I'll call an Enemy from Outside, a foe of the spirit, is about. On my breast there was a feeling of heat as if I'd been burnt by a match. It was where I wore Betty's gift. The cross too was warning me. Then, two dim spots of yellow phosphorescence glowed at a height even with mine. A hard sound like a hoof striking a stone echoed once.

This was enough for Bran! With a squeal of fright which sounded more like a hare than a blood horse, he turned and bolted. If I had not freed my hands I would have been thrown off in an instant, and as it was I had the very devil of a time staying on. He was not merely galloping, but bounding, gathering his quarters under him with each stride as if to take a jump. Only sheer terror can make a trained horse so forget himself.

I did my best to guide him, for through the night I heard the golden questing note of a horn. The Wild Hunt was drawing the coverts. They seemed to be quite far down the valley and fortunately Bran was running away across its upper part, in the same direction as the Big House.

I caught a glimpse of its high, lightless gables, black against the stars as we raced over some open ground a quarter mile below it, then we were in the trees again, and I finally began to master the horse, at length bringing him to a halt. Once again, as he stood, sweated and shivered, I used my ears. At first there was nothing, then, well down the vale to my right front came the sound of the questing horn. I was still undiscovered.

You may wonder, as I did at first, why I had heard no hounds. Surely it would have been easy for this crew to keep some bloodhounds, or perhaps smear my clothes or horse with anise and use their own thoroughbred fox hounds. I can only say I don't know. At a guess, and mind you, it's only a guess, there were other powers or elements loose that night which might have come into conflict with a normal hunting pack. But that's only a guess. Still, there were none, and though I was not yet sure of it, I was fairly certain, for even the clumsiest hound should have been in full cry on my track by now. The Wild Hunt then, seemed to hunt at sight. Again the clear horn note sounded. They were working up the slope in my direction.

As quietly as possible, I urged Bran, who now seemed less nervous, along the edge of the little wood we were in and down the slope. We had galloped from the hill spur on the right, as one faced away from the house, perhaps two thirds of the way across the valley, which at this point was some two miles wide. Having tried one slope and met—well, whatever I *had* met, I would not try the other.

My first check came at a wooden fence. I didn't dare jump such a thing at night, as much for the noise as for the danger of landing badly. But I knew there were gates. I dismounted and led Bran along until I found one, and then shut it carefully behind me. I had not heard the mellow horn note for some time and the click of the gate latch sounded loud in the frosty night. Through the large field beyond I rode at a walk. There was another gate at the far side, and beyond that another dark clump of wood. It was on the edge of this that I suddenly drew rein.

Ahead of me, something was moving down in the wood. I heard some bulky creature shoulder into a tree trunk and the sound of heavy steps. It might have been another horse from the sound. But at the same moment, up the slope behind me, not too far away, came the thud of hooves on the ground, many hooves. The horn note blew, not more than two fields away, by the sound. I had no choice and urged Bran forward into the trees. He did not seem too nervous, and went willingly enough. The sound ahead of me ceased and then, as I came to a tiny glade in the heart of the little wood, a dim shape moved ahead of me. I checked my horse and watched, knife ready.

"Donald?" came a soft voice. Into the little clearing rode Betty, mounted on a horse as dark as mine, her great black mare. I urged Bran forward to meet her.

"I've been looking for you for over an hour," she whispered, her breath warm on my cheek. I was holding her as tightly as I could, our mounts standing side by side, amiably sniffing one another. "Let me go, Donald, or we'll both be dead. There's a chance, a thin one, if we go the way I've thought out." She freed herself and sat looking gravely at me. My night vision was good and I could see she had changed into a simple tunic of what looked like doeskin and soft, supple knee boots. Socketed in a sling was one of the short, heavy spears and I reached over and took it. The very heft of it made me feel better. The glimmering blade seemed red even in the dim tree light and I suddenly realized the point was bronze. These extraordinary people went in for authenticity in their madness.

"Come on, quickly," she said and wheeled her horse back the way she had come. I followed obediently and we soon came to the edge of the forest. Before us lay another gentle slope, but immediately beneath us was a sunken dirt road, which meandered away to the left and downhill between high banks, their tops planted with hedge. We slid down a sandy slope and our horses began to walk along the road, raising hardly any dust. Betty rode a little ahead, her white face visible as she turned to look back at intervals. Far away a cock crowed, but I looked at my watch and it was no more than 3 A.M. I could hear nothing uphill and the horn was silent. We rode through a little brook, our path crossing it at a pebbly ford only inches deep. Then, as we had just passed out of hearing the gurgle of the stream, a new sound broke the quiet night.

It was somewhere between a whinny and a screech and I remembered the noise I had heard as the two riders had driven me through the hedge. If one could imagine some unthinkable horse-creature screaming at the scent of blood—eagerly, hungrily seeking its prey, well, that's the best I can do to describe it.

"Come on, we have to ride for our lives!" Betty hissed. "They have let the Dead Horse loose upon us. No one can stand against that."

With that, she urged her mount into a gallop and I followed suit. We tore along the narrow track between the banks, taking each twist at a dead run, always angling somehow downhill and toward the valley mouth.

Then, the road suddenly went up and I could see both ahead and behind. Betty reined up and we surveyed our position. At the same time the horn blew again, but short, sharp notes this time and a wild screaming broke out. Three fields back up the long gentle slope the Wild Hunt had seen our black outlines on the little swell where we paused. I could see what looked like a dozen horsemen coming full tilt and the faint glitter of the spears. But Betty was looking back down along our recent track.

From out of the dark hollows came a vast grunting noise, like that of a colossal pig sighting the swill pail. It was very close.

Betty struck her horse over the withers and we started to gallop again in real earnest. Bran was tired, but he went on nobly, and her big mare simply flew. The Hunt was silent now, but I knew they were still coming. And I knew too that something else was coming. Almost, I felt a cold breath on my back, and I held the spear tightly against Bran's neck.

Suddenly, Betty checked, so sharply her horse reared, and I saw why as I drew abreast. We had come very close to the mouth of the valley and a line of fires lay before us, not three hundred yards away on the open flat. Around them moved many figures, and even at this distance I could see that a cordon was established and from the hats and glint of weapons, I knew not by the Waldrons or their retainers. Apparently the outside world was coming to Waldrondale, at least this far. We had a fighting chance.

Between us and the nearest fire, a black horseman rode at us, and he was only a hundred feet off. The raised spear and the bare head told me that at least one of the valley maniacs had been posted to intercept me, in the unlikely event of my getting clear of the rest.

I spurred the tired hunter forward and gripped the short spear near its butt end, as one might a club. The move was quite instinctive. I knew nothing of spears but I was out to kill and I was a six-goal polo player. The chap ahead, some Waldron cousin, I expect, needed practice, which he never got. He tried to stab at me overhand, but before our horses could touch I had swerved and lashed out as I would on a long drive at the ball. The heavy bronze edge took him between the eyes and really, that was that. His horse went off to one side alone.

Wheeling Bran, I started to call to Betty to come

on and as I did saw that which she had so feared
had tracked us down.

I am still not entirely certain of what I saw, for
I have the feeling that part of it was seen with what
Asiatics refer to as the Third Eye, the inner "eye"
of the soul.

The girl sat, a dozen yards from me, facing something which was advancing slowly upon us. They
had called it the Dead Horse, and its shifting outlines indeed at moments seemed to resemble a mon-
strous horse, yet at others, some enormous and
distorted pig. The click of what seemed hooves was
clear in the night. It had an unclean color, an oily
shifting, dappling of gray and black. Its pupilless
eyes, which glowed with a cold, yellow light, were
fixed upon Betty, who waited as if turned to stone.
Whatever it was, it had no place in the normal scheme
of things. A terrible cold again came upon me and
time seemed frozen. I could neither move nor speak,
and Bran trembled, unmoving between my legs.

My love broke the spell. Or it broke her. God
knows what it must have cost her to defy such a
thing, with the breeding she had, and the training.
At any rate, she did so. She shouted something I
couldn't catch, apparently in that pre-Gaelic gib-
berish they used, and flung out her arm as if striking
at the monster. At the same instant it sprang, straight
at her. There was a confused sound or sounds, a
sort of *spinning*, as if an incredible top were whirling
in my ear, and at the same instant my vision blurred.

When I recovered myself, I was leaning over Bran's
neck, clutching him to stay on, and Betty lay silent

in the pale dust of the road. A yard away lay her horse, also unmoving. And there was nothing else.

As I dismounted and picked her up, I knew she was dead, and that the mare had died in the same instant. She had held the thing from Outside away, kept it off me, but it had claimed a price. The high priestess of the cult had committed treason and sacrilege and her life was the price. Her face was smiling and peaceful, the ivory skin unblemished, as if she were asleep.

I looked up at the sound of more galloping hoof-beats. The Wild Hunt, all utterly silent, were rounding a bend below me and not more than a hundred yards away. I lifted Betty easily, for she was very light, and mounted. Bran still had a little go left and we headed for the fires, passing the dead man lying sprawled in his kilt or whatever on the road. I was not really afraid any longer and as I drew up at the fire with a dozen gun barrels pointed at me, it all felt unreal. I looked back and there was an empty hill, a barren road. The riders of Waldron-dale had vanished, turned back apparently at the sight of the fires and the armed men.

"He's not one; look at the gal! That crowd must have been hunting *him*. Call the parson over or Father Skelton, one of you. Keep a sharp lookout, now!"

It was a babble of voices and like a dream. I sat down, staring stupidly and holding Betty against my heart until I realized a man was pulling at my knees and talking insistently. I began to wake up then, and looking down, recognized the minister I had seen the previous day. I could not remember his name but I handed Betty down to him when he asked, as obediently as a child.

"She saved me, you know," I said brightly. "She left them and saved me. But the Dead Horse got her. That was too much, you see. She was only a girl, couldn't fight *that*. You do see, don't you?" This is what I am told I said at any rate, by Mr. Andrews, the Episcopal minister of the little Church of the Redeemer. But that was later. I remember none of it.

When I woke, in the spare bed of the rectory the next day, I found Andrews sitting silently by my bed. He was looking at my bare breast on which lay the little Celtic cross. He was fully dressed, tired and unshaven and he reeked of smoke, like a dead fireplace, still full of coals and wood ash.

Before I could speak, he asked me a question. "Did she, the young lady, I mean, give you that?"

"Yes," I said. "It may have saved me. Where is she?"

"Downstairs, in my late wife's room. I intend to give her a Christian burial, which I never would have dreamed possible. But she has been saved to us."

"What about the rest of that crowd?" I said. "Can nothing be done?"

He looked calmly at me. "They are all dead. We have been planning this for three years. That Hell spawn have ruled this part of the country since the Revolution. Governors, senators, generals, all Waldrons, and everyone else afraid to say a word."

He paused. "Even the young children were not saved. Old and young, they are in that place behind the house. We took nothing from the house but your clothes. The hill folk who live to the west came down on them just before dawn, as we came up. Now there is a great burning: the house, the groves, everything. The State Police are coming but several bridges are out for some reason, and they will be quite a time." He fell silent, but his eyes gleamed. The prophets of Israel were not all dead.

Well, I said a last goodbye to Betty and went back to Washington. The police never knew I was there at all, and I was apparently as shocked as anyone to hear that a large gang of bootleggers and Chicago gangsters had wiped out one of America's first families and gotten away clean without being captured. It was a six-day sensation and then everyone forgot it. I still have the little cross, you know, and that's all.

They'll Never Find You Now

DOREEN DUGDALE

Hidden behind the thick hedge, Sweeney studied the cottage and the old woman pottering in its garden.

The dilapidated cottage seemed to be fighting a losing battle with the encroaching vegetation. Small wonder if the bent old woman who was snipping at flowers and shrubs was the only gardener.

Sweeney had come across the place only by accident, having taken a wrong turning and landed himself in a maze of winding and ever-narrowing lanes. When the stolen mini had suddenly acquired a puncture he had pushed it off the road into a thicket, taken his suitcase and, cursing his bad luck, gone forward on foot.

The lane had been knobbly as a knuckleduster under his thin city shoes, and he had seen no habitation of any kind until he had come upon the cottage.

The old woman hobbled back indoors with her basket of cuttings, and the only remaining sign of life was a large black cat sunning itself on the door-step.

Sweeney shuffled his aching feet and weighed the pros and cons. All his instincts told him the woman lived alone—he could scent loneliness and defenselessness as quickly as he could smell a peeled orange—and he had to hide somewhere for a while.

Cautiously Sweeney followed the hedge round to the back. There was another neglected strip of garden with a nanny goat tethered to a post and a few hens scratching about in a wire run. Self-sufficient this old girl—and Sweeney reckoned she needed to be, living as she did in such isolation. He made up his mind; the cottage might be a bit short on the mod. cons., but it offered safety.

His double cross would have been discovered by now and the gang would be searching for him. They would never find him here, that was certain. He would wait long enough for them to think he had slipped through the net and got out of the country, then he would make his way down to the coast where the fisherman who had ferried Vickie across the channel was waiting to make a second trip with him.

Sweeney sweated a little as he thought of Vickie—blonde, beautiful, and waiting for him to join her with the proceeds of the robbery. Not just his share but the whole of the cash. She was worth the risk he had taken but he valued his neck too much to spoil everything for want of a bit of patience now.

He picked up his case and went round to the

front again. The cat, seeing him come up the path, stretched itself lazily and slipped ahead of him into the cottage.

Sweeney stood in the doorway, his big frame blocking out the light, and stared assessingly around. The room was cluttered but comparatively clean and had a pleasant, gardenlike perfume from bunches of mint, thyme, and other herbs which hung drying from the mantelshelf.

The old woman had frozen into an animal stillness, her hands motionless amongst the blossoms spread on the table. She was even older than he had thought, just skin and bones. Only her bright, monkey-brown eyes showed any vitality.

"Good afternoon," Sweeney said, playing it cool. "May I use your phone?"

"There is no phone here." The voice was a rusty croak.

"Well, maybe your husband or son could give me a hand to get the car back on the road?"

She shook her head. "There is nobody but me here."

Sweeney reached behind him and closed the cottage door.

The woman's hand fluttered to her throat. "What do you want?"

"Just board and lodging for a while." Sweeney nodded towards an ancient sofa. "That will do if you haven't got a spare bed."

The old eyes studied Sweeney's face, registering its brutality and the bleak coldness of his prominent, heavy-lidded eyes.

"Nobody would want to stay here . . . unless they were trying to hide."

"That's about it, Grandma." He was moving about the room, opening drawers and cupboards. They contained nothing but an eccentric old country-woman's collection of junk. There was nothing to make him doubt that she lived alone.

"Are the police looking for you?"

Sweeney grinned. "Yeah, them too—but it's more my friends I'm concerned about at the moment. If they get their hands on me after what I've done. . . ." His grin vanished and he gripped the old woman's shoulder, making her wince. "Do you have any vis-itors here? The truth now—or I'll make you regret it."

She surprised him with a cackle of laughter. "Vis-itors? Who'd want to visit me? There is not a soul within miles."

"That's what I thought. How come you live here all on your own like this?"

"I was born here." All at once she seemed to accept Sweeney's presence as inevitable. "There were other cottages scattered around here then. But times change. There is only me left now. Me and Blackie."

The cat, which had been sitting quietly at her feet, looked up and acknowledged its name with a soft mew.

Sweeney sat down in one of the two fireside chairs, the suitcase full of money placed carefully within reach.

Just so that the old girl should know the score right from the start, he took his revolver out of his pocket and examined it nonchalantly. Fear flickered in the woman's eyes and Sweeney put the gun away again casually, as if it had been a cigarette lighter.

"I want food and a place to sleep. You won't come to any harm so long as you do as you are told—but don't cross me, see?"

She nodded and returned to her sorting of flowers and leaves. Her gnarled hands were trembling but she obviously wasn't the hysterical type. That suited Sweeney. He didn't want to have to knock her about—she was too frail to stand up to it and he couldn't afford to have that complication along with everything else.

Time, Sweeney decided a couple of hours later, was going to be his biggest problem here. It was going to drag so much it would drive him up the wall with boredom. The old woman didn't even have a radio let alone television.

Sweeney pushed his plate away and sat picking his teeth disconsolately. His meal had been surprisingly good—an omelet made with eggs fresh from the hens and fragrant with herbs, accompanied by homemade bread and cheese. He had realized that his unwilling hostess must be some sort of back-to-nature crank—but he didn't mind going back to nature if it resulted in food that tasted like that.

But how was he going to kill time? He saw himself cooped up in the cottage, perhaps for weeks, with not even a drink to relieve the monotony—and suddenly the hideout didn't seem such a good idea after all.

He went out to the little scullery where the old woman, who had said she would have her own meal later, tended a pot bubbling on the stove.

It was a mystery to Sweeney how she could cook so well on anything so ancient. Flames leaped and spluttered from its rusty iron top, filling the place with a scarlet glow.

"Hell." Sweeney's voice was truculent. "I don't suppose you have even got a drink in this Godforsaken hole!"

The old woman looked at him in silence for a moment, then shuffled across to open a cupboard door.

Sweeney, glimpsing bottles of homemade wines, pushed her aside and began rummaging. Beetroot, dandelion, elderberry, and, more to his fancy, a bottle labeled "sloe gin."

"Get me a glass," Sweeney ordered, and took the bottle back with him to the big fireside chair.

"That's strong stuff, Grandma!" Sweeney nodded his approval. The gin was as smooth as silk but with a kick like dynamite.

For the first time since his arrival the old woman smiled.

"In the old days," she boasted, "people used to come from miles around for my sloe gin—and other things I used to make for them."

"I can believe it." Sweeney refilled his glass. Once again he found himself thinking how monkeylike the old woman's eyes were—bright, and with a kind of sly mischievousness lurking in their brown depths.

He could have snapped her in two with his bare

hands, he told himself, but it was always as well to be cautious. He placed his gun to hand on the table.

"Drunk or sober, I can put a bullet in you," he said. "So don't get any ideas."

"An old woman like me?" She looked at him for a moment, then went out to the scullery again.

Sweeney smiled and refilled his glass. The cottage was quite cozy at night with the firelight flickering on the copper kettle and brass fire irons.

"I've done all right for myself," Sweeney said, addressing the cat curled up in the chair opposite.

"What's that you are cooking, Ma?" Sweeney could see the old woman bent over the pot oblivious to the steam wreathing about her face.

"Oh, just a pinch of this and a scrap of that." The rusty old voice seemed to come from far away.

"Smells good," Sweeney said and he was amused to hear himself having trouble pronouncing the words. His glass was empty so he filled it again and drank in silence for a while. He had begun to feel quite lethargic although drink didn't usually affect him that way.

He watched the cat uncurl itself and arch its back in a long, luxurious stretch. It began purring and, with its emerald eyes fixed on Sweeney, it clawed at the chair cushion, moving its paws one after the other in a soft, padding, feline kind of dance.

Sweeney shook his head, trying to clear it. The old woman was singing in the scullery, her voice cracked and shrill.

"Shut up," Sweeney said. But the old woman took no notice, just went on stirring the pot and chanting—it wasn't really singing—and despite his be-mused senses Sweeney was chillingly aware that he didn't like the words.

The cat's purring grew louder, a rumbling accompaniment to its mistress's chant.

Sweeney tried to rise from his chair but found that he couldn't. He felt so . . . peculiar. A kind of strange disturbance was taking place within him—a kaleidoscopic rearrangement of molecule and cell.

The old woman came in from the scullery, the cat stopped its purring, and together they looked at the small green frog with the protuberant eyes so like Sweeney's that squatted now in Sweeney's chair.

"Come along, little 'un," the old woman said. She carried the frog to the front door and placed it on the step. It stayed still, its bulging eyes gazing mournfully upwards, until she put her foot under its head and flipped it onto the path—then it went hopping off into the undergrowth.

"That's it, my dear, off you go," said the old woman. "And if it's any consolation—they'll never find you now."

The Widow Flynn's Apple Tree

LORD DUNSANY

These are two stories, though they tell of the same event. The first is Sergeant Ryan's story, given on oath before the magistrate who was trying the case of young Micky Maguire, a lad of sixteen, for stealing the apples of the widow Flynn, and damaging her apple tree to the extent of one and threepence. And the second is Micky Maguire's story. I will give Sergeant Ryan's story first, and I will call the attention of the reader to the fact that it was given on oath. He said:

"In consequence of information received I went to the garden of the widow Flynn at nine P.M. on the night of November the second and saw the prisoner, whom I later identified as Micky Maguire, lying under her apple tree unconscious, with a broken branch in his hand on which were eight apples, the breaking off of which I estimated damaged the tree to the extent of one and threepence. I subsequently revived him with cold water, which I applied to his face, and he appeared to be suffering from concussion, as was later diagnosed by Dr. Murphy. The widow Flynn made no charge against him and did not answer my questions (being apparently much concerned with the state of the health of the accused), but the branch with the eight apples on it was in his hand when I first saw him. The apples were not his own property."

The magistrate then asked Micky Maguire if he had anything to say in his defense, or if he wished to question Sergeant Ryan. Micky Maguire did not wish to question the sergeant, but spoke at some length in his defense; and this is the second story.

"I did not go to the widow Flynn's garden to steal her apples. I did not go to her garden at all till she went there with me. I went to her door, and knocked at it and asked if I might come in. I went after dark only because I am working all day and could not go then, and when I had done my work I had my tea, and then I went down to see the widow Flynn in her house beside the bog, which is some way from the town, as your honor knows; and it grew dark before I got there.

"I went to see her because I had been reading old tales about Ireland, and I had read how people that had the power to do it used to be turning princes into wild swans; and I wanted to know if there was anyone could do that now, or if all the old tales were over and the Ireland they told of gone for ever. And by reason of what they do say about the widow Flynn I thought that, if anyone had the power yet, she would be the one to have it. And so, when she asked me what I wanted, I asked if there was anyone had the power now to turn princes into swans; not meaning her particularly, but asking if there was anyone that could do it. And she said maybe there were, but she hadn't heard of them.

"She had certain powers herself, she said; and I said to her: 'Sure, I know you have, Mrs. Flynn.' But she said these times were not the old times, and she couldn't turn princes into wild swans, but maybe she might turn an ordinary young lad into a goose. And I said: 'That will do well for me, Mrs. Flynn; for I'll know the old times are not all gone if you can do that, nor the old Ireland.' And then she made some incantations and said some spells; and I'd say what they were, for it's the truth I'm telling, your honor, only she swore me not to, by a very terrible oath, and you'd not have me break that."

"No, no, no," said the magistrate. "Just tell us in your own words what happened after that."

"Well," said Micky Maguire, "when she swore me, I swore her, and I swore her to turn me back to a man again whenever I came to her, and she swore to do that whenever I came. 'But it might not be so easy to come, Mrs. Flynn,' I said to her, 'with all the young lads about here that have guns. What supposing one of them was down by the bog looking for geese? If I lighted down in front of your door he might get me.'

" 'You needn't touch earth at all,' she said. 'Come within thirty yards of me and I can cast a spell over you, and you'll be a man again at once.'

"And I got her oath on that. And then she let rip with her incantations and, whether your honor believes it or not, sure there I was a gray lag. Well, I was frightened a bit for a moment and nearly thought of asking her to make me a man again at once. But I soon saw that that was not what I had come for, so I just spread my wings and found flying as easy as walking. Aye, and easier. I had got up into the old woman's apple tree before she turned me, so as to give myself a start, and it is the widow Flynn herself that recommended it; and I sailed away over the bog from out of the apple tree. Aye, I sailed away over the bog. I was a gray lag all right. And a grand thing it is, your honor, to feel the wind in your wings and to know that the air is a high road for you. But I didn't go far, for I didn't know where to go, and thought I'd better ask."

"Whom did you ask?" said the magistrate. "Can you bring him here to corroborate what you're saying?"

"Sure I asked the geese," said Micky. "They were down on the bog. Whom else would I ask?"

"Yes, yes," said the magistrate. "Go on."

"They were down on the bog feeding. And I began to feel hungry myself. Indeed, I was hungry most of the time I was with them, for they don't have two or three meals in the day, same as us, and then have done with it, but they're eating whenever they've nothing else to do; and I was a goose now and I'd got the ways of them, and I felt hungry."

"And what did you eat?" asked the magistrate.

"Ah, it was nothing your honor would ever have noticed," said Micky.

"I don't care whether I've noticed it or not," said the magistrate. "But I must have facts by which to test your evidence; and I'm asking you what you ate."

"Sure, it was only a thing called briskauns," said Micky Maguire, "a bulb that does be growing down by the bog. One grubs it up with one's beak, and your honor would never believe how good it was."

"What does it taste like, this bulb?" asked the magistrate.

"Like stout and oysters," said Micky. "Sure, the geese went mad for it; and, being a goose now, I was just as eager to get it myself."

"And then?" said the magistrate.

"Then I asked them the way to the North," said Micky, "for I knew they would be going about this time, and I wanted to see the world. And they told me that when it was time to go, there would be a wind rising up from the bog, and one went up with that into the clear sky; and that was not the wind that would take one to the North, but when one got up there one found the wind waiting. That was what they said, and I found it was true when the time came. But that time was not yet, for it was early in the month of November and they'd only just come South. Well, I won't tell your honor, what your honor knows already, of the habits of the geese of Drumahooley."

"Listen to me," said the magistrate. "The more

you tell me what I know already, the better for you; for if any of it is like anything that I ever heard before, I may find some truth in it. Just try if you can to tell a plain tale, as Sergeant Ryan has done."

"I will, sir," said Micky. "Well, we grazed the fields that lie round Drumahooley bog by day, with a sentry out all the time to look out for robbers and murderers. I mean, saving your presence, foxes and men. And just as it got dark we used to fly into the bog, going wide past the big willow that your honor knows, at the western edge of it, because that's the best cover for a lad with a gun, and it's where anyone would go; so we used to keep out of shot of it. It wasn't I that told them about that; they knew all about it themselves. There was nothing that I could tell them about anything that they didn't know already. And a great deal they told me that I never knew and that your honor wouldn't believe, so that there's no use saying any of it in my defense.

"There was a lady of the geese there that told me a great deal. She told me of the journey to the North before we went; and so wonderful her tale of it sounded that I thought I would tell her something wonderful too, and I told her how I was a man that had been enchanted; but she said that there was nothing in that at all, for that she was a princess whose father had reigned in Ireland nine hundred years ago, and an enchantment had been put on her for a thousand years by a witch.

"Well, I talked of a lot of things that might seem silly to your honor, and she told me a lot of the old history of Ireland. And, if I was to tell your honor all she told me of that, it would take the whole day; and it is not part of my defense. And she told me things she knew of the ancient wisdom of the geese. And they know more of the earth we walk and the sky over us than ever I would have thought of, but it's hard for me to put it into words; it was just a feeling that they had for everything in the earth and among the winds, and knowing what all of them would do; when the snow would fall and when the young oats would come up, and all the things that were going to happen, which we hardly notice, or not the way they notice it.

"Well, winter came, and the bog froze for a week, as your honor may remember. And we went away to the streams, when we knew that the frost was coming; and I mayn't tell your honor what streams we went to, for it is one of the secrets of the geese, but there's many here that can corroborate me when I say that we did go; and we came back after the end of that week. And then as the winter wore away there began to be great talk about the North; they were all talking of it, and any time a wind arose on the bog there would always be one of them wondering if that was the wind, the one that was to take us up. But it wasn't yet, for the young green oats were not yet come up; and it is a tradition among the geese that they never go to the North till they have had one feed on green oats.

"And the green oats came up, and we had a great feed on them when they were about two inches high, in the field to the west of the bog that is owned by Patrick O'Donahue, a great feed; and the day after that the wind came. It riz up suddenly when we were out on the bog, and the leader just lifted his head and we were all off at once. It had been getting too warm lately, and there was a listless feeling all over the fields, and the North was calling. So we slanted up with the wind and away we went."

"What date was all this?" asked the magistrate.

"Sure, that is the trouble," said Micky. "They don't keep the same kind of dates that we do, so I can't tell your honor."

"But did all this happen on the day that Sergeant Ryan deposes to having found you in Mrs. Flynn's garden?"

"Sure, I don't know," said Micky. "It was a different kind of time altogether."

"In this Court," said the magistrate, "you must go by the right time. Which reminds me. Why isn't that clock going? Finnegan, have it attended to. Well, go on, Maguire."

And Maguire went on. "We went up on that wind and got amongst big clouds where we could scarcely see each other for a while, but only heard our voices. But soon we came to a valley among the clouds, that was made by the wind we were riding; and we went up through that and came out at the top of them, and the clouds were all shining beneath us. Well, I saw then, what I never thought of before, that a goose gets nearer to Heaven than even a man gets; I mean, till his immortal soul parts from him altogether. And it didn't seem that Heaven could be much higher, nor yet a great deal more beautiful. If it's made of solid gold it has those clouds beat, but it would take pure gold to do it."

"I never allow religion or politics in this Court," said the magistrate.

"I beg your honor's pardon," said Micky. "Well, we were above the clouds, as I was saying, and they were tinted a little with gold; and there were rifts among them the same as we have valleys down here; and through the valleys we had glimpses of Ireland, looking very small and queer; you couldn't tell a wood from a patch of rushes, or a hill from a mound of earth that had been thrown up by a spade and gone green. There was an old fellow flying in front of us to show the way to the North, and we spread out in two lines behind him to left and right. And so we went on over the hills and fields and bogs, and even over towns, for at that height there was no harm in them. Sometimes the clouds closed in and we saw nothing but that lovely land that lies between earth and Heaven; and then the valleys came in them again, and we saw streams running down at the foot of the valleys, and in some odd way, your honor, these streams seemed to have cut a way for themselves through the clouds, as they had through the earth; and I don't know how that is, but I'm telling your honor the honest truth."

"Yes, yes," said the magistrate. "I'm not more surprised at one part of your story than another. But it's my duty to hear all you may have to say in your defense. Go on."

"Well, your honor, everything down there was looking very small; and then we came to the sea. And we could see right to the bottom of it where the currents were sleeping, and there were long lines of seaweed where the currents had left them; they were a dark mauve, your honor, and the sea was all green. And night came while we were over the sea, and we were still going northward."

"Did you steer by the stars?" asked the magistrate.

"We did not," said Micky. "We steered by an old knowledge the leader had, which he may have got from the stars or the winds or the witches; but, however it was, it was just an old knowledge he had, for after several years I became the leader myself and I had that knowledge and I led the flock by it, and there may have been stars in it, but how I came by it I never knew, nor what it was made of."

"Several years? Several years?" said the magistrate. "Dear me. But on what date do you say all this started?"

"Amn't I after telling your honor," said Micky, "that there is a different time with the geese, and different dates? And I can't say what date it was."

"Do you deny the date given by Sergeant Ryan?"

"Sure, I do not," said Micky. "I don't deny any date. Only the time is all different."

"Well, go on," said the magistrate.

"We came to the gray cliffs," said Micky, "and the inlets of the sea; and a bright, clear wind was roaring, and we had come to the North. And we dipped, and the clouds came raging past us, but their shadows on the green land were only moving lazily."

"I don't see how that could be," said the magistrate.

"I am thinking it was our own pace," said Micky, "that made the clouds seem to go by so fast, and that there wasn't all that hurry in them at all. But, however that may be, the shadows weren't hurrying. And we came down into those blessed lands. And I don't like to be saying it to your honor, for I have nothing against any man, but the reason those lands were so blessed was that no man ever came there. Blessed indeed they were, and the daylight lingered there, till I almost thought at first that the sun would never set; it was almost as if we were so near to Heaven that we had touched the edge of eternity. Grand clean winds blew there with no taint of smoke in them, and none of the new noises."

"What do you mean by the new noises?" asked the magistrate.

"I mean the noises since man appeared on the earth," said Micky, "and since cities were built, and especially the last hundred and fifty years or so; and the geese say it's getting worse every year. It was a grand, clean wind with a taste of salt in it, and the noises were all the old noises that are a part of creation, so that they never disturbed us while we slept, or worried us while we waked. It was the blessed land, the land of peace. And yet there came a time when the call of Ireland began to stir in our hearts, as there had stirred the call of the North. And when that came we looked for the wind again, watching for it among the grasses on which we were grazing. And one day it rose up from among the flowers, and we went with it and we came South again, steering by our old knowledge of winds and stars, and something more than that.

"And this went on for years, but I won't be taking up any more of your honor's time. But one day the enchantment left the princess of the House of Ireland and she went from among us, the thousand years being up before their time, or she having miscalculated the date. But it was only a miscalculation, for she never told me a lie. And when that happened I said to myself: Sure, I'll go too. And the moment we came South, which was in the first days of November, I left the flock as they slanted down to the bog, and I came down straight from the stars to where I could see the roof of the widow Flynn's house, all black in the fields. And I remembered what she told me, that if ever I came within thirty yards of her she would disenchant me, as she had sworn to do. And I called out to her with the cry of a goose, and sailed backwards and forwards low over her roof.

"I hadn't gone over her roof three times, when she knew it was me, and came running out and made her incantations, as she had sworn she would. But there was one thing the old woman never thought of; and I can't blame her either, for I never thought of it myself; for she disenchanted me in the air, and I became a man again. And, as your honor knows, a man can't fly; and I came crashing down and, if it hadn't been for the old woman's apple tree, which broke my fall, I'd have been killed altogether, and wouldn't be here at all to take up the time of your honor. Sure, that's how it all was."

"And what does the widow Flynn say?" asked the magistrate.

"Sure, she'll say nothing," said Sergeant Ryan. "And maybe it might be better not to be troubling that kind of old woman at all."

"I see," said the magistrate. "Very well. Well, Maguire, I have listened to all you had to say in your defense, and I am not casting any reflection whatever on the evidence deposed to by Sergeant Ryan. You must understand that. At the same time I consider that you have perhaps been punished enough by your fall from the apple tree. So I find you not guilty."

And that is the end of the two stories of the damage to the widow Flynn's apple tree.

In the Cards

JOHN COLLIER

The Vascal System is the most reliable, the most up-to-date, and the most scientific method of fore-telling the future by cards. It is true the operator cannot tell his own fortune, but that drawback seems to be common to all methods, and in every other way the successes of the Vascal System have been prodigious.

A wife, who studied Vascal in her spare time, laid out the cards for her husband on the breakfast table. She revealed to him that he would be involved in an unfortunate collision, and suffer a severe shock at the very least, if by any chance he drove his car home between three and five that afternoon. He now regularly desires his wife to lay out the cards for him, and never drives home before the hours she announces as propitious, with the result that he is almost the only person in the whole neighborhood who has not been considerably shocked during the period in question.

A young girl, holder of a Grade-A Vascal Diploma, was able to warn her still younger sister that she might that evening expect to lose something she had possessed all her life, through the agency of a tall, dark man, but though this would cause her some little distress at the outset, it would in the end lead to lasting happiness and satisfaction. Sure enough, the young sister left for a blind date that evening in such haste that she forgot to lock the door behind her. A tall, dark sneak thief, entering, took away her baby seed-pearl necklace, which was a tatty little number anyway, and she was successful in gypping the insurance people for at least three times its value, and bought that very same rhinestone clip which first attracted the attention of Mr. Jerry Horrabin, now her fiancé.

Mr. Brewster, when only halfway through the Vascal Course, laid out the cards for his wife, and told her she would be wrong to insist on going to the theater that evening, because the show would stink. She did insist, and it did stink.

Convinced by these, and by scores of other unsolicited testimonials, Myra Wilkins decided she could hardly do better than enroll as a student. Her idea was a big one—she meant to play her cards properly. She considered that, sooner or later, among the numerous young men who would flock to consult her, she would strike one for whom she could foresee an enormous fortune arriving in the near future from some unsuspected source. She had no intention of unsettling this happy young man by telling him what the future held, but thought rather she might warn him against any Queens of Hearts or Diamonds with whom he might be involved, and guide him gently toward a marriage with a high-grade Spade, for Myra was a brunette.

She graduated with the highest honors, and set up in a shadowy little nook in the West Forties, above the establishment of a dancing instructress with whom she was acquainted. She figured that young men who took dancing lessons often had a great yearning to know what the future held for them, and she hoped these would form the nucleus of a clientele.

Myra had very little capital, and this was exhausted in furnishing her nook with bead curtains, witch balls, images of Buddha, and similar junk, to create a convincing atmosphere for her visitors. She set her fee very low, in order to get the widest possible range of clients, and thus increase her chances of finding a future millionaire among them.

She shuffled and spread her greasy pack of cards, foretelling for innumerable insignificant young men the details of futures that were little better than pasts, which of course they would become one of these days. As far as the imminent fortune was concerned, the whole business was like a game of solitaire that never came out. The average future wealth of her clients was somewhere about the Two of Diamonds, and work and worry loomed up like a straight flush in clubs or spades.

The months stretched on into years, and the dust lay thick upon the witch ball and the Buddha. Myra had nothing but her dreams of wealth, and these, like an old knife, were sharpened to a razor keenness. At last, late one afternoon, when the shadows were at their deepest, the stairway groaned beneath a heavy tread, and a hulking figure tried to get four ways at once through the bead curtain that screened her alcove.

The new customer was an ugly one, and a more prosperous fortuneteller would probably have sent him straight back to the zoo. Myra, however, could not afford to pass up a dollar, so she wearily laid out her pack. The Two of Clubs frisked around fairly actively in the near foreground, in a context which gave it the significance of a cop's nightstick. She saw that her client was in some danger of visiting a large building, full of men in strange clothes, but vaguer influences seemed to indicate a postponement of this necessity.

Suddenly she had to repress a cry that rose unbidden to her lips. It was as if his future, dark as a cannibal king, had smiled, and revealed a golden tooth. Vascal declared unequivocally that a handsome fortune was coming to this young man on the death of someone very near to him.

"Have you any relations?" she asked. "Any near relations, I mean, who are well off?"

"No," said he. "Not unless Uncle Joe soaked anything away before they got him."

"That must be it," she thought. "Well," she said aloud, "it doesn't matter much. There's no sign of any uncle leaving you anything. This card means money troubles. This means you're double-crossed by a blonde. Looks like you're beaten up, too. I don't know what these two men in uniform are doing."

She continued prattling and laying out the cards, her mind working meanwhile like a three-ring circus. One ring was taken up with the story she was telling to her visitor, the second in reading the real future as it unfolded itself, and the third in wondering what she was going to do about it.

She stole another glance at her unattractive client. The fortune, as far as she could judge, appeared to be rather more than a million. Her visitor, on the other hand, seemed a good deal less than human. Myra had not expected romance, but there are things which make a nice girl hesitate, and he was one of them.

While she pondered, she was still automatically laying out the cards. Suddenly, her eyes brightened. She looked again. It was true. All her troubles were ended. The cards indicated, beyond the shadow of a doubt, that her client would die of a sudden, violent shock within a few months of inheriting the money. This made quite an eligible bachelor of him.

Myra at once began her maneuvers. "You seem," she said, "to be at the parting of the ways. One road leads to misery, poverty, sickness, despair, prison . . ."

"I'll take the other," said the young man.

"You show great powers of judgment," said Myra. "But, I can tell you, it is not as easy as all that. The other road, which leads to riches and happiness, can be traveled only hand-in-hand with a good woman. Do you know a good woman?"

"Oh, phooey!" said her client in dismay.

"What a pity!" said Myra. "Because, if you did, and if she was dark, and not bad-looking, and wore a number-five shoe, all you'd have to do would be to marry her, and you'd be rich for life. Very rich. Look—here it is. Money, money, money—coming to you from someone very near to you. If you marry the right girl, that is. Look—this card means you at the Waldorf. Look—this is you at Palm Beach. Here you are at Saratoga. Gosh! You've backed a big winner!"

"Say, lady," said her client. "What size shoe do *you* wear?"

"Well," said Myra with a smile, "I *can* squeeze into a four. But, usually . . ."

"Look, baby," said he, taking her hand. "It's you and me. Like that. See?" With that, he extended his other hand with two fingers crossed, as an emblem of connubial bliss.

Myra controlled a shudder. "When he's dead," thought she, "I'll have a million, and get me one of these young film stars, in order to forget!"

Soon afterwards they were married, and took a small shack in an unprepossessing part of Long Island. Lew appeared to have strong reasons for living in inconspicuous retirement. Myra commuted, and drudged harder than ever with her greasy pack of cards in order to keep them both until death did them part, leaving her a rich widow.

As time went on, and the fortune still failed to materialize, she was bitterly reproached by her hulking husband, whose stunted mind was as impatient as a child's, and who began to fear he had been married under false pretenses. He was also a little sadistic.

"Maybe you ain't the right dame after all," said he, pinching her black and blue. "Maybe you don't wear a five. Maybe you wear a six. Gimme a divorce and let me marry another dark dame. The money don't come along, and you're black and blue anyway. I don't like a black and blue dame. Come on, gimme a divorce."

"I won't," said she. "I believe marriages are made in Heaven."

This would lead to an argument, for he claimed to have evidence to the contrary. In the end, his brutish wits would be baffled; he would fling her to the ground with a curse, and go into the backyard, where he would dig an enormously deep hole, into which he would gaze for a long time, and then fill it in again.

This continued for some months, and Myra herself began to wonder if the Vascal System could possibly have let her down. "Supposing he doesn't come into the money. Here I am—Mrs. King Kong, and working for it! Maybe I'd better get that divorce after all."

These defeatist notions came to a head one gloomy winter evening as she trudged home from the ferry. Crossing the dark yard of the shack, she stumbled into another of the enormous holes dug by her simpleminded husband. "That settles it," thought she.

When she entered the squalid kitchen, Lew greeted her with an unusual smile. "Hello, sweetie," said he. "How's my darling little wifie tonight?"

"Cut the sweetie stuff out," said she tersely. "And the wifie stuff, too. I don't know what's bit you, you big gorilla, but my mind's made up. You can have that divorce, after all."

"Don't talk like that, honey," said he. "I was only joking. I wouldn't divorce you, not for all the world."

"No, but I'll divorce you," said she. "And quick."

"You gotta have grounds for that," observed her husband, with a frown.

"I've got 'em," said she. "When I show that judge where I'm black and blue, I'll get my divorce pronto. I'm sitting pretty."

"Listen," said he. "Have a look at this letter that came for you. Maybe you'll change your mind."

"Why did you open my letter?" said Myra.

"To see what was inside," said he with the utmost candor. "Go on, read it."

"Uncle Ezra," cried Myra, staring at the letter. "Left a million and a half dollars! All to me! Gee, the old geezer must have made good! But, say, the cards must have slipped up, then. It was supposed to come to you."

"Never mind," said Lew, stroking the back of her neck. "Man and wife are one, ain't they?"

"Not for long," cried Myra in triumph. "I'm rich! I'm free! Or, I will be."

"And what shall *I* do?" asked her husband.

"Go climb a tree," said Myra. "You ought to be good at it."

"I thought you might say that," said he, clasping her firmly around the throat. "Gypped me a dollar for that fortune, too, didn't you? Well, if you won't do right by me, the cards must. Death of someone very near to me—that's what they said, didn't they? So they was right after all!"

Myra had no breath left to thank him on behalf of the Vascal System, or to warn him of the sudden, violent shock that awaited him.

Strangers in Town

SHIRLEY JACKSON

I don't gossip. If there is anything in this world I loathe, it is gossip. A week or so ago in the store, Dora Powers started to tell me that nasty rumor about the Harris boy again, and I came right out and said to her if she repeated one more word of that story to me I wouldn't speak to her for the rest of my life, and I haven't. It's been a week and not one word have I said to Dora Powers, and that's what I think of gossip. Tom Harris has always been too easy on that boy anyway; the young fellow needs a good whipping and he'd stop all this ranting around, and I've said so to Tom Harris a hundred times and more.

If I didn't get so mad when I think about that house next door, I'd almost have to laugh, seeing people in town standing in the store and on corners and dropping their voices to talk about fairies and leprechauns, when every living one of them knows there isn't any such thing and never has been, and them just racking their brains to find new tales to tell. I don't hold with gossip, as I say, even if it's about leprechauns and fairies, and it's my held opinion that Jane Dollar is getting feeble in the mind. The Dollars weren't ever noted for keeping their senses right up to the end anyway, and Jane's not older than her mother was when she sent a cake to the bake sale and forgot to put the eggs in it. Some said she did it on purpose to get even with the ladies for not asking her to take a booth, but most just said the old lady had lost track of things, and I dare say she could have looked out and seen fairies in her garden if it ever came into her mind. When the Dollars get that age, they'll tell anything, and that's right where Jane Dollar is now, give or take six months.

My name is Addie Spinner, and I live down on Main Street, the last house but one. There's just one house after mine, and then Main Street kind of runs off into the woods—Spinner's Thicket, they call the woods, on account of my grandfather building the first house in the village. Before the crazy people moved in, the house past mine belonged to the Bartons, but they moved away because he got a job in the city, and high time, too, after them living off her sister and her husband for upward of a year.

Well, after the Bartons finally moved out—owing everyone in town, if you want my guess—it wasn't long before the crazy people moved in, and I knew they were crazy right off when I saw that furniture.

I already knew they were young folks, and probably not married long because I saw them when they came to look at the house. Then when I saw the furniture go in I knew there was going to be trouble between me and her.

The moving van got to the house about eight in the morning. Of course, I always have my dishes done and my house swept up long before that, so I took my mending for the poor out on the side porch and really got caught up on a lot I'd been letting slide. It was a hot day, so I just fixed myself a salad for my lunch, and the side porch is a nice cool place to sit and eat on a hot day, so I never missed a thing going into that house.

First, there were the chairs, all modern, with no proper legs and seats, and I always say that a woman who buys herself that flyaway kind of furniture has no proper feeling for her house—for one thing, it's too easy to clean around those little thin legs; you can't get a floor well-swept without a lot of hard work. Then, she had a lot of low tables, and you can't fool me with them—when you see those little low tables, you can always tell there's going to be a lot of drinking liquor going on in that house; those little tables are made for people who give cocktail parties and need a lot of places to put glasses down. Hattie Martin, she has one of those low tables, and the way Martin drinks is a crime. Then when I saw the barrels going in next door, I was sure. No one just married has that many dishes without a lot of cocktail glasses, and you can't tell me any different.

When I went down to the store later, after they

were all moved in, I met Jane Dollar, and I told her about the drinking that was going to go on next door, and she said she wasn't a bit surprised because the people had a maid. Not someone to come one day a week and do the heavy cleaning—a maid. Lived in the house and everything. I said I hadn't noticed any maid, and Jane said most things if I hadn't noticed them she wouldn't believe they existed in this world, but the Wests' maid was sure enough; she'd been in the store not ten minutes earlier buying a chicken. We didn't think she'd rightly have time enough to cook a chicken before suppertime, but then we decided that probably the chicken was for tomorrow, and tonight the Wests were planning on going over to the inn for dinner and the maid could fix herself an egg or something. Jane did say that one trouble with having a maid— Jane never had a maid in her life, and I wouldn't speak to her if she did—was that you never had anything left over. No matter what you planned, you had to get new meat every day.

I looked around for the maid on my way home. The quickest way to get to my house from the store is to take the path that cuts across the back garden of the house next door, and even though I don't use it generally—you don't meet neighbors to pass the time of day with, going along a back path—I thought I'd better be hurrying a little to fix my own supper, so I cut across the Wests' back garden. West, that was their name, and what the maid was called I didn't know, because Jane hadn't been able to find out. It was a good thing I did take the path, because there was the maid, right out there in the garden, down on her hands and knees, digging.

"Good evening," I said, just as polite as I could. "It's kind of damp to be down on the ground."

"I don't mind," she said. "I like things that grow."

I must say she was a pleasant-speaking woman, although too old, I'd think, for domestic work. The poor thing must have been in sad straits to hire out, and yet here she was just as jolly and round as an apple. I thought maybe she was an old aunt or something and they took this way of keeping her, so I said, still very polite, "I see you just moved in today?"

"Yes," she said, not really telling me much.

"The family's name is West?"

"Yes."

"You might be Mrs. West's mother?"

"No."

"An aunt, possibly?"

"No."

"Not related at all?"

"No."

"You're just the maid?" I thought afterward that she might not like it mentioned, but once it was out I couldn't take it back.

"Yes." She answered pleasant enough, I will say that for her.

"The work is hard, I expect?"

"No."

"Just the two of them to care for?"

"Yes."

"I'd say you wouldn't like it much."

"It's not bad," she said. "I use magic a lot, of course."

"Magic?" I said. "Does that get your work done sooner?"

"Indeed it does," she said with not so much as a smile or a wink. "You wouldn't think, would you, that right now I'm down on my hands and knees making dinner for my family?"

"No," I said. "I wouldn't think that."

"See?" she said. "Here's our dinner." And she showed me an acorn, I swear she did, with a mushroom and a scrap of grass in it.

"It hardly looks like enough to go around," I said, kind of backing away.

She laughed at me, kneeling there on the ground with her acorn, and said, "If there's any left over, I'll bring you a dish; you'll find it wonderfully filling."

"But what about your chicken?" I said; I was well along the path away from her, and I did want to know why she got the chicken if she didn't think they were going to eat it.

"Oh, that," she said. "That's for my cat."

Well, who buys a whole chicken for a cat, that shouldn't have chicken bones anyway? Like I told Jane over the phone as soon as I got home, Mr. Honeywell down at the store ought to refuse to sell it to her or at least make her take something more fitting, like ground meat, even though neither of us believed for a minute that the cat was really going to get the chicken, or that she even had a cat, come to think of it; crazy people will say any-thing that comes into their heads.

I know for a fact that no one next door ate chicken that night, though; my kitchen window overlooks their dining room if I stand on a chair, and what they ate for dinner was something steaming in a big brown bowl. I had to laugh, thinking about that acorn, because that was just what the bowl looked like—a big acorn. Probably that was what put the notion in her head. And, sure enough, later she brought over a dish of it and left it on my back steps, me not wanting to open the door late at night with a crazy lady outside, and like I told Jane, I certainly wasn't going to eat any outlandish con-coction made by a crazy lady. But I kind of stirred it around with the end of a spoon, and it smelled all right. It had mushrooms in it and beans, but I couldn't tell what else, and Jane and I decided that probably we were right the first time and the chicken was for tomorrow.

I had to promise Jane I'd try to get a look inside to see how they set out that fancy furniture, so next morning I brought back their bowl and marched right up to the front door—mostly around town we go in and out back doors, but being as they were new and especially since I wasn't sure how you went about calling when people had a maid, I used the front—and gave a knock. I had gotten up early to make a batch of doughnuts, so I'd have something to put in the bowl when I took it back, so I knew that the people next door were up and about because I saw him leaving for work at seven-thirty. He must have worked in the city, to have to get off so early. Jane thinks he's in an office, because she saw him going toward the depot, and he wasn't running; people who work in offices don't have to get in on the dot, Jane said, although how she would know I couldn't tell you.

It was little Mrs. West who opened the door, and I must say she looked agreeable enough. I thought with the maid to bring her breakfast and all she might still be lying in bed, the way they do, but she was all dressed in a pink house dress and was wide awake. She didn't ask me in right away, so I kind of moved a little toward the door, and then she stepped back and said wouldn't I come in, and I must say, funny as that furniture is, she had it fixed up nice, with green curtains on the windows. I couldn't tell from my house what the pattern was on those curtains, but once I was inside I could see it was a pattern of green leaves kind of woven in, and the rug, which of course I had seen when they brought it in, was green too. Some of those big boxes that went in must have held books, because there were a lot of books all put away in bookcases, and before I had a chance to think I said, "My, you must have worked all night to get everything arranged so quick. I didn't see your lights on, though."

"Mallie did it," she said.

"Mallie being the maid?"

She kind of smiled, and then she said, "She's more like a godmother than a maid, really."

I do hate to seem curious, so I just said, "Mallie must keep herself pretty busy. Yesterday she was out digging your garden."

"Yes." It was hard to learn anything out of these people, with their short answers.

"I brought you some doughnuts," I said.

"Thank you." She put the bowl down on one of those little tables—Jane thinks they must hide the wine, because there wasn't a sight of any such thing that I could see—and then she said, "We'll offer them to the cat."

Well, I can tell you I didn't much care for that. "You must have quite a hungry cat," I said to her.

"Yes," she said. "I don't know what we'd do without him. He's Mallie's cat, of course."

"I haven't seen him," I said. If we were going to talk about cats, I figured I could hold my own, having had one cat or another for a matter of sixty years, although it hardly seemed a sensible subject for two ladies to chat over. Like I told Jane, there was a lot she ought to be wanting to know about the village and the people in it and who to go to for hardware and what not—I know for a fact I've put a dozen people off Tom Harris's hardware store since he charged me seventeen cents for a pound of nails—and I was just the person to set her straight on the town. But she was going on about the cat. "—fond of children," she was saying.

"I expect he's company for Mallie," I said.

"Well, he helps her, you know," she said, and then I began to think maybe she was crazy too.

"And how does the cat help Mallie?"

"With her magic."

"I see," I said, and I started to say goodbye fast, figuring to get home to the telephone, because people around the village certainly ought to be hearing about what was going on. But before I could get to the door the maid came out of the kitchen and said good morning to me, real polite, and then the maid said to Mrs. West that she was putting together the curtains for the front bedroom and would Mrs. West like to decide on the pattern? And while I just stood there with my jaw hanging, she held out a handful of cobwebs—and I never did see anyone before or since who was able to hold a cobweb pulled out neat, or anyone who would want to, for that matter— and she had a blue jay's feather and a curl of blue ribbon, and she asked me how I liked her curtains.

Well, that did for me, and I got out of there and ran all the way to Jane's house, and of course, she never believed me. She walked me home just so she could get a look at the outside of the house, and I will be everlastingly shaken if they hadn't gone and put up curtains in that front bedroom, soft white net with a design of blue that Jane said looked like a blue jay's feather. Jane said they were the prettiest curtains she ever saw, but they gave me the shivers every time I looked at them.

It wasn't two days after that I began finding things. Little things, and even some inside my own house. Once there was a basket of grapes on my back steps, and I swear those grapes were never grown around our village. For one thing, they shone like they were covered with silver dust, and smelled like some foreign perfume. I threw them in the garbage, but I kept a little embroidered handkerchief I found on the table in my front hall, and I've got it still in my dresser drawer.

Once I found a colored thimble on the fence post, and once my cat, Samantha, that I've had for eleven years and more, came in wearing a little green collar and spat at me when I took it off. One day I found a leaf basket on my kitchen table filled with hazelnuts, and it made me downright shaking mad to think of someone's coming in and out of my house without so much as asking, and me never seeing them come or go.

Things like that never happened before the crazy people moved into the house next door, and I was telling Mrs. Acton so, down on the corner one morning, when young Mrs. O'Neil came by and told us that when she was in the store with her baby she met Mallie the maid. The baby was crying because he was having a time with his teething, and Mallie gave him a little green candy to bite on. We thought Mrs. O'Neil was crazy herself to let her baby have candy that came from that family and said so, and I told them about the drinking that went on and the furniture getting arranged in the dark and the digging in the garden, and Mrs. Acton said she certainly hoped they weren't going to think that just because they had a garden they had any claim to be in the Garden Club.

Mrs. Acton is president of the Garden Club. Jane says I ought to be president, if things were done right, on account of having the oldest garden in town, but Mrs. Acton's husband is the doctor, and I don't know what people thought he might do to them when they were sick if Mrs. Acton didn't get to be president. Anyway, you'd think Mrs. Acton had some say about who got into the Garden Club and who didn't, but I had to admit that in this case we'd all vote with her, even though Mrs. O'Neil did tell us the next day that she didn't think the people could be all crazy, because the baby's tooth came through that night with no more trouble.

Do you know, all this time that maid came into the store every day, and every day she bought one chicken. Nothing else. Jane took to dropping in the store when she saw the maid going along, and she says the maid never bought but one chicken a day. Once Jane got her nerve up and said to the maid that they must be fond of chicken, and the maid looked straight at her and told her right to her face that they were vegetarians.

"All but the cat, I suppose," Jane said, being pretty nervy when she gets her nerve up.

"Yes," the maid said, "all but the cat."

We finally decided that he must bring food home from the city, although why Mr. Honeywell's store wasn't good enough for them I couldn't tell you. After the baby's tooth was better, Tom O'Neil took them over a batch of fresh-picked sweet corn, and they must have liked that, because they sent the baby a furry blue blanket that was so soft that young Mrs. O'Neil said the baby never needed another, winter or summer, and after being so sickly, that baby began to grow and got so healthy you wouldn't know it was the same one, even though the O'Neils never should have accepted presents from strangers, not knowing whether the wool might be clean or not.

Then I found out they were dancing next door. Night after night after night, dancing. Sometimes I'd lie there awake until ten, eleven o'clock, listening to that heathen music and wishing I could get up the nerve to go over and give them a piece of my mind. It wasn't so much the noise keeping me from sleeping—I will say the music was soft and kind of like a lullaby—but people haven't got any right to live like that. Folks should go to bed at a sensible hour and get up at a sensible hour and spend their days doing good deeds and housework. A wife ought to cook dinner for her husband—and not out of cans from the city, either—and she ought to run over next door sometimes with a home-baked cake to pass the time of day and keep up with the news. And most of all a wife ought to go to the store herself, where she can meet her neighbors and not just send the maid.

Every morning I'd go out and find fairy rings on the grass, and anyone around here will tell you that means an early winter, and here next door they hadn't even thought to get in coal. I watched every day for Adams and his truck because I knew for a fact that cellar was empty of coal; all I had to do was lean down a little when I was in my garden and I could see right into the cellar, just as swept and clear as though they planned to treat their guests in there. Jane thought they were the kind who went off on a trip somewhere in the winter, shirking responsibilities for facing the snow with their neighbors. The cellar was all you could see, though. They had those green curtains pulled so tight against the windows that even right up close there wasn't a chink to look through from outside, and them inside dancing away. I do wish I could have nerved myself to go right up to that front door and knock some night.

Now, Mary Corn thought I ought to. "You got a right, Addie," she told me one day in the store. "You got every right in the world to make them quiet down at night. You're the nearest neighbor they got, and it's the right thing to do. Tell them they're making a name for themselves around the village."

Well, I couldn't nerve myself, and that's the gracious truth. Every now and then I'd see little Mrs. West walking in the garden, or Mallie the maid coming out of the woods with a basket—gathering acorns, never a doubt of it—but I never so much as nodded my head at them. Down at the store I had to tell Mary Corn I couldn't do it. "They're foreigners, that's why," I said. "Foreigners of some kind. They don't rightly seem to understand what a person says—it's like they're always answering some other question you didn't ask."

"If they're foreigners," Dora Powers put in, being at the store to pick up some sugar to frost a cake, "it stands to reason there's something wrong to bring them here."

"Well, I won't call on foreigners," Mary said.

"You can't treat them the same as you'd treat regular people," I said. "I went inside the house, remember, although not as you might say to pay a call."

So then I had to tell them all over again about the furniture and the drinking—and it stands to reason that anyone who dances all night is going to be drinking too—and my good doughnuts from my grandmother's recipe going to the cat. And Dora, she thought they were up to no good in the village. Mary said she didn't know anyone who was going to call, not being sure they were proper, and then we had to stop talking because in came Mallie the maid for her chicken.

You would have thought I was the chairman of a committee or something, the way Dora and Mary kept nudging me and winking that I should go over and speak to her, but I wasn't going to make a fool of myself twice, I can tell you. Finally Dora saw there was no use pushing me, so she marched over and stood there until the maid turned around and said, "Good morning."

Dora came right out and said, "There's a lot of people around this village, miss, would like to know a few things."

"I imagine so," the maid said.

"We'd like to know what you're doing in our village," Dora said.

"We thought it would be a nice place to live," the maid said. You could see that Dora was caught up short on that, because who picks a place to live because it's nice? People live in our village because they were born here; they don't just come.

I guess Dora knew we were all waiting for her, because she took a big breath and asked, "And how long do you plan on staying?"

"Oh," the maid said, "I don't think we'll stay very long, after all."

"Even if they don't stay," Mary said later, "they can do a lot of harm while they're here, setting a bad example for our young folk. Just for instance, I heard that the Harris boy got picked up again by the state police for driving without a license."

"Tom Harris is too gentle on that boy," I said. "A boy like that needs a whipping and not people living in a house right in town showing him how to drink and dance all night."

Jane came in right then, and she had heard that all the children in town had taken to dropping by the house next door to bring dandelions and berries from the woods—and from their own fathers' gardens, too, I'll be bound—and the children were telling around that the cat next door could talk. They said he told them stories.

Well, that just about did for me, you can imagine. Children have too much freedom nowadays anyway, without getting nonsense like that into their heads. We asked Annie Lee when she came into the store, and she thought somebody ought to call the police on them, so it could all be stopped before somebody got hurt. She said, suppose one of those kids got a step too far inside that house—how did we know he'd ever get out again? Well, it wasn't too pleasant a thought, I can tell you, but trust Annie Lee to be always looking on the black side. I don't have much dealing with the children as a rule, once they learned they'd better keep away from my apple trees and my melons, and I can't say I know one from the next, except for the Martin boy I had to call the police on once for stealing a piece of tin from my front yard, but I can't say I relished the notion that that cat had his eyes on them. It's not natural, somehow.

And don't you think it was the very next day that they stole the littlest Acton boy? Not quite three years old, and Mrs. Acton so busy with her Garden Club she let him run along into the woods with his sister, and first thing anyone knew they got him. Jane phoned and told me. She heard from Dora, who had been right in the store when the Acton girl came running in to find her mother and tell her the baby had wandered away in the woods, and Mallie the maid had been digging around not ten feet from where they saw him last. Jane said Mrs. Acton and Dora and Mary Corn and half a dozen others were heading right over to the house next door, and I better get outside fast before I missed something, and if she got there late to let her know everything that happened. I barely got out my own front door when down the street they came, maybe ten or twelve mothers, marching along so mad they never had time to be scared.

"Come on, Addie," Dora said to me. "They've finally done it this time."

I knew Jane would never forgive me if I hung back, so out I went and up the front walk to the house next door. Mrs. Acton was ready to go right up and knock, because she was so mad, but before she had a chance the door opened and there was Mrs. West and the little boy, smiling all over as if nothing had happened.

"Mallie found him in the woods," Mrs. West said, and Mrs. Acton grabbed the boy away from her; you could tell they had been frightening him by the way he started to cry as soon as he got to his own mother. All he would say was "kitty," and that put a chill down our backs, you can imagine.

Mrs. Acton was so mad she could hardly talk, but she did manage to say, "You keep away from my children, you hear me?" And Mrs. West looked surprised.

"Mallie found him in the woods," she said. "We were going to bring him home."

"We can guess how you were going to bring him home," Dora shouted, and then Annie Lee piped up, from well in the back, "Why don't you get out of our town?"

"I guess we will," Mrs. West said. "It's not the way we thought it was going to be."

That was nice, wasn't it? Nothing riles me like people knocking this town, where my grandfather built the first house, and I just spoke up right then and there.

"Foreign ways!" I said. "You're heathen wicked people, with your dancing and your maid, and the sooner you leave this town, the better it's going to be for you. Because I might as well tell you"—and I shook my finger right at her—"that certain people in this town aren't going to put up with your fancy ways much longer, and you would be well advised— very well advised, I say—to pack up your furniture and your curtains and your maid and cat and get out of our town before we put you out."

Jane claims she doesn't think I really said it, but all the others were there and can testify I did—all but Mrs. Acton, who never had a good word to say for anybody.

Anyway, right then we found out they had given the little boy something, trying to buy his affection, because Mrs. Acton pried it out of his hand, and he was crying all the time. When she held it out, it was hard to believe, but of course with them there's nothing too low. It was a little gold-colored apple, all shiny and bright, and Mrs. Acton threw it right at the porch floor, as hard as she could, and that little toy shattered into dust.

"We don't want anything from you," Mrs. Acton said, and as I told Jane afterward, it was terrible to see the look on Mrs. West's face. For a minute she just stood there looking at us. Then she turned and went back inside and shut the door.

Someone wanted to throw rocks through the windows, but, as I told them, destroying private property is a crime and we might better leave violence to the menfolks, so Mrs. Acton took her little boy home, and I went in and called Jane. Poor Jane; the whole thing had gone off so fast she hadn't had time to get her corset on.

I hadn't any more than gotten Jane on the phone when I saw through the hall window that a moving van was right there next door, and the men were starting to carry out that fancy furniture. Jane wasn't surprised when I told her over the phone. "Nobody can get moving that fast," she said. "They were probably planning to slip out with that little boy."

"Or maybe the maid did it with magic," I said, and Jane laughed.

"Listen," she said, "go and see what else is going on—I'll hang on the phone."

There wasn't anything to see, even from my front porch, except the moving van and the furniture coming out; not a sign of Mrs. West or the maid.

"He hasn't come home from the city yet," Jane said. "I can see the street from here. They'll have news for him tonight."

That was how they left. I take a lot of the credit for myself, even though Jane tries to make me mad by saying Mrs. Acton did her share. By that night they were gone, bag and baggage, and Jane and I went over the house next door with a flashlight to see what damage they left behind. There wasn't a thing left in that house—not a chicken bone, not an acorn—except for one blue jay's wing upstairs, and that wasn't worth taking home. Jane put it in the incinerator when we came downstairs.

One more thing. My cat, Samantha, had kittens. That may not surprise you, but it sure as judgment surprised me and Samantha, her being over eleven years old and well past her kitten days, the old fool. But you would have laughed to see her dancing around like a young lady cat, just as light-footed and as pleased as if she thought she was doing something no cat ever did before; and those kittens troubled me.

Folks don't dare come right out and say anything to me about my kittens, of course, but they do keep on with that silly talk about fairies and leprechauns. And there's no denying that the kittens are bright yellow, with orange eyes, and much bigger than normal kittens have a right to be. Sometimes I see them all watching me when I go around the kitchen, and it gives me a cold finger down my back. Half the children in town are begging for those kittens—"fairy kittens," they're calling them—but there isn't a grownup in town would take one.

Jane says there's something downright uncanny about those kittens, but then Jane would even gossip about cats, and I may never speak to her again in all my life. She won't tell me what folks are saying about my kittens, and gossip is one thing I simply cannot endure.

The Proof

JOHN MOORE

The two men who watched her took turn and turn about. Toward evening the tall scowling one came back, and the short fat one who had yawned on the hard bench for two or three hours got up respectfully. "Nothing has entered," he said. Just then a bee buzzed at the open window, and the scowling man, whom she knew as Matthew Hopkins, strode swiftly across the room to examine it. The other followed him, and together they watched the bee intently until it flew away.

"Only a bumble," said the short fat man.

"Nevertheless I have known them take the form of insects," said Mr. Hopkins. He added sharply: "You have to keep your wits about you in this business."

"Yes, sir."

"Birds and animals are more usual," Mr. Hopkins went on. He quoted some Latin which she did not understand, and she guessed that the short man, although he tried to look very wise, didn't understand it either. Mr. Hopkins, however, translated for his benefit. "Owls and bats and cats are especially favored, but insects are not unheard of, by any means. Night moths and chafers for instance. And even slugs."

"Yes, sir."

"Even slugs," repeated Mr. Hopkins darkly. "So remember to keep your eyes open always. You may go now; I will watch. Dusk is their favorite hour." He sat down on the bench and stared with his pale wild eyes toward the window.

Now at last she began to understand what they were about. At first she had been so bewildered and frightened that she thought they had tied her cross-legged to the stool as part of her punishment. Sooner or later, surely, they would let her go and she would creep back to her cottage and shut the door against the gossiping neighbors and try to forget the shame and the indignities which had been put upon her. But now she realized that this new ordeal was merely a continuation of the trial: they were waiting and watching for her Familiar Spirit, or something of the kind, to come through the window. Well, they could wait for that till Domesday; for she was no witch, and despite her weariness and her cramp and the pain of the cords which bound her so tightly she still had enough assurance and confidence left to be angry.

"You can wait till Domesday," she said aloud. But the scowling man with the pale eyes took no notice;

he did not even shift his stare from the window, and her own words sounded strange in the quiet room. She bit her lip, wishing she had not spoken.

It was best, she told herself, to keep silent; for they twisted your own words against you, as she had discovered that morning when they took her before the magistrate and accused her of things which she had never imagined or dreamed of. She had answered with spirit, and Mr. Hopkins had said with a conventional shrug of his shoulders: "You see, sir, how the Devil puts these pert replies into the woman's mouth?"

"Confine your answers to yes and no," said the magistrate; and Mr. Hopkins began to cross-examine her again.

"Were you or were you not in love with the young man called Reuben Taylor?"

"Yes," she said at last. It was no use denying it, the whole neighborhood had known it. Alas, she had worn her heart upon her sleeve!

"And did not his mother oppose the match?"

"Yes."

"And did you or did you not, on his mother's doorstep, in the hearing of several God-fearing and respectable persons, put a curse upon his mother, because she would not let you go in to see him when he lay dying?"

"It wasn't a curse! I knew he was ill, and within the house I could hear him calling for me, and—and I was so distressed I didn't know what I said."

Mr. Hopkins pounced on her like some swift beast. *"So you knew he was ill?"*

"Everybody knew."

"Yes or no," said Mr. Hopkins.

"Yes."

"And then he died?" said Mr. Hopkins.

She bowed her head. It was two years ago, and the world had been empty ever since, yet she had never cried until now. She did not easily cry. But suddenly tears came and she hid her face, so that she scarcely heard the things which Mr. Hopkins was saying to the magistrate nor troubled to deny the meaningless questions he put to her: Was she aware that Mother Taylor's dun cow had died on the first of March 1644 of an unaccountable milk fever? Did she not know that the pied cow had died on the 15th of the same affliction? And the roan cow on the 2nd of April? "Oh, what do I care about cows!" she cried, with all the grief and loneliness of twenty-four months lapping about her. "The milk, sir," went on Mr. Hopkins inexorably, "is said to have curdled in their udders, which thereupon mortified."

At last the magistrate said:

"I find a *prima facie* case. Mr. Hopkins, you may proceed with your examination."

They took her then to another room in the Town Hall, but the crowd followed and clamored at the door so loudly that Mr. Hopkins had to let them in; and at least a dozen people were pressing about her when the short fat man suddenly pinioned her arms behind her back and Mr. Hopkins lifted her skirt and pressed a pin into her thigh. She scarcely felt the prick, for she was faint with terror and shame. "Ho, ho, a presentable witch," said a coarse voice in the crowd. "She bleeds, she bleeds," said somebody else, and Mr. Hopkins let her skirt fall. "The Devil has many artifices," he said. "It is therefore proper to decide these matters not upon one fallible test, but upon many." He began to make much of a small wart which she had on her wrist, and a mole on her forearm. She could scarcely bear the touch of his questing fingers on her skin, and she cried out in protest:

"I have had it since childhood."

"Aye, aye," scowled Mr. Hopkins, "maybe your Master put it as a mark upon ye, as a shepherd burns a brand upon his sheep. We will proceed nevertheless to a further experiment." It was then they bound her to the stool in the middle of the room, opened the window, and drove out the inquisitive crowd. The Watching began.

The light from the sinking sun now came slanting through the narrow window in a thin beam which fell between her and her watcher. Somehow it reminded her of a flaming sword, and made her think of angels, from which thought she drew comfort for a while, for surely God would not let them find her guilty of these things which she had never done? So she prayed, but silently, lest Mr. Hopkins should hear her and think she prayed to the Devil and not to God. "Make them let me go," she said, and repeated it again and again, so that soon she almost persuaded herself that when night came they would untie the cords and allow her to scurry back to her cottage just up the lane. For a few moments her faith was so strong that she shut her eyes and actually saw herself unlatching the green door and going inside among all her friendly and familiar things, the spinning-wheel in the corner, the kettle on the hob, the brown milk-jug on the table. And Tibb would be crying for her milk, for it was past supper-time—Tibb, whose eyes grew as round and as luminous as moons in the rushlight; Tibb, jumping onto her shoulder and rubbing a soft head against her face.

The thought of Tibb's purring welcome gave her comfort, for during the last two lonely years she had lavished all her pent-up love on the small black cat. At least Tibb would not shun her as the neighbors had shunned her today, when she was being led through the streets and had called out in vain for someone to come and testify on her behalf. They had turned away, and some of them had mocked her; inquisitive heads peering out of windows had been swiftly withdrawn. Once she had heard, or thought she had heard, a bloodchilling cry of "Burn her! Burn her!" She had never felt so alone as she did then, knowing that the only one who would have spoken for her lay in the churchyard at the top of the hill. So now in her loneliness and misery her thoughts turned to the black cat, and behind her shut eyelids she saw Tibb playing the absurd game which they played together every evening, when she would crook her fingers in front of the light so that a shadow fell upon the wall, now of a bird with flapping wings, now of a rabbit with twitching ears. Then Tibb with arched back and hackles raised

would mince before the shadows, adding to them
the tantalizing reflection of her own tail; to and fro,
to and fro, prancing, leaping, scrabbling up the wall
in pursuit of the unattachable phantom, her lunar
eyes ablaze with the weird pale light that was neither
yellow nor green. And so the game went on, until
both were tired and they went up the creaking stairs
to bed.

Perhaps she dozed, in spite of her cramped position and the cruel cords; for surely she dreamed
that she was in bed, and safe, and felt in her dreams
the pressure of Tibb's small body stirring at her
feet. But suddenly a queer sound, a dry crackling
flutter, startled her and made her open her eyes.
The beam from the window was much paler now,
it was no longer like a flaming sword, but the specks
of dust still danced in it, and through it, as through
a piece of thin gauze, she saw her watcher crouch
as if he were about to spring. At the same moment
a moving shadow fell across the beam, there was a
swish of wings, and Mr. Hopkins leaped toward the
window. His leap was all the more terrifying because she did not know the reason for it; she
screamed, and then the beam was clear once more
and she saw the bat for a second as it fluttered away
against the pale evening sky. Mr. Hopkins went
slowly back to the bench and resumed his watching.

She did not close her eyes again, but sat taut and
upright, straining against the cords, with all her
nerves atingle. For the first time she fully understood her danger. Her assurance ebbed away from
her. It was true enough that she was no witch and

possessed no Familiar Spirit—ah, but *what if something did enter the room while they watched her?* What if the bat had blundered in? Or even the bee?

She prayed again, but with less confidence: "Please, God, don't let anything come in." Panic came nearer with the gathering darkness, for the beam from the window had faded altogether and the darkness crouched in all the four corners of the room like the blurred figure of Mr. Hopkins crouched on his bench: like him, it waited to spring. The smallest sound made her pounding heart beat faster—even the ping of a mosquito, which Mr. Hopkins scowled upon as if he suspected that even such an atomy might conceal the Devil. Outside, the barn owl which lived in the apple tree halfway down the lane began his evening hunting, and because she was still young, and had sharp ears, she could hear what Mr. Hopkins couldn't—the slate-pencil squeaking of the bats as they hawked for flies. She remembered what Mr. Hopkins had said to the short fat man who seemed to be his assistant: "Owls and bats and cats are especially favored."

And cats! Her heart thumped again as she remembered Tibb. By now, surely, Tibb would be hungry and crying for her supper, stalking about the cottage and down the garden-path, only a hundred yards away, looking for her mistress who had never failed to feed her before. What if Tibb—? But no, that was impossible, dogs would follow a person—to the ends of the earth, it was said—but cats were different: their strange unfathomable little minds were centered upon a hearth; like lonely spinsters they worshiped household gods. So she reasoned, and was able to calm herself a little. Tibb would not seek her, nor in any case know where to find her. As for the bats and the owls, they were creatures of the sky; why should she imagine that they might blunder into a room—and through this particular window, of all the windows in the town?

Nothing would come in, she told herself. In the morning they would let her go.

And then she heard the cat mewing. She didn't know which came first—the very faint, distant mewing, or the recollection that she had screamed when the bat's shadow fell across the sunbeam. But as soon as she heard that tiny cry, halfway between a mew and a chirrup, she recognized it as the answer which Tibb always gave when she called her, and she realized that Tibb had heard her screams.

Mr. Hopkins, motionless on the bench, made no sign; and even when the mewing came nearer he did not stir. Perhaps even now Tibb would fail to find her and would go back to the cottage up the lane. She strove to quieten her breathing, and held it until the blood surged and thundered in her ears. When at last she was compelled to let it go, it came in short choking gasps, so loud that Mr. Hopkins turned his head to stare at her.

She saw him stiffen. "*Ah*," he said. "The Devil begins to manifest himself."

There was a sound so slight that it might have been the stirring of the evening wind and suddenly she saw Tibb on the windowsill, framed against the pale square of sky. For a second Tibb paused there, ears pricked, hackles raised, tail curved over the arched back; and then with a little chirrup Tibb jumped and the duck-egg-blue square was empty again, the cat was on her lap purring and rubbing its head against her, and she was tugging frantically against the cords which bit into her wrists, perhaps to stroke it, perhaps to push it away.

Mr. Hopkins did not leap this time. He rose very slowly from the bench and came toward her. Almost wearily, without triumph and without surprise. *"Probatum est,"* he said. "It is proved."